THE MISSING THIEF

An enthralling crime mystery full of twists

(Yorkshire Murder Mysteries Book 9)

ROGER SILVERWOOD

JOFFE BOOKS

Revised edition 2020
Joffe Books, London
www.joffebooks.com

First published as "The Curious Mind of Inspector Angel" 2007

ISBN: 978-1-78931-312-3

ONE

Sheffield, South Yorkshire, UK. Thursday, 14 December 1940. 11.50 p.m.

It was the first night of the Sheffield blitz in World War II. Stick after stick of bombs had brought death and destruction to the city centre. Houses, hotels, factories and shops had been reduced to piles of rubble in minutes. Only skeletons of some buildings remained standing; some were on fire. The sky was yellow and the air tasted of sulphur.

The poor people of Sheffield had not experienced anything like it. The continuous boom, boom, boom of exploding bombs disturbed the mind as well as the ears. Those who had been caught outside in the raids were scurrying to shelter in hotel basements or any below-ground level cover they could find. Many streets, roads and pavements were impassable. Buses, taxis and cars were left abandoned. In places, the smell of burning timber and dust filled the air. Fire engines and tenders were trying to reach fires but could not always reach their objective because of the heavy piles of stones across the roads. Ambulances were crammed full of the standing wounded on their way to the hospitals, which were themselves damaged in the onslaught. The police were out in force doing whatever they could to protect the people and their property.

A lone policeman, PC Shaw, was standing in Fitzalan Square in front of what had been the Marples Hotel, which was now a shell. Several small fires were emanating from what remained of the ground floor. Shaw had just pulled a man out of a bed that had been blown into the street, and managed to find a place for him in an ambulance and assist it on its way, when he saw a canvas-sided 15-cwt Morris van with a green flag fastened to its windscreen rocking towards him over a heap of stones. As he shone his torch at the vehicle, he could see that it was a khaki army vehicle and that it had battalion flashes on its front. There were two men in it. It shuddered and stopped quite close to him. One of the men got out and rushed towards him. PC Shaw saw that he was a uniformed army officer wearing RAOC flashes and had three pips up. His dust covered hand was carrying a few sheets of paper fastened at the corner with a paper clip.

'Ah! Excuse me, Constable,' the officer shouted above the barrage.

'Yes, sir?' Shaw said and shone his torch on him.

'I have to get to Liverpool first thing tomorrow morning. I don't seem to be able to get out of the city,' he said loudly and pushed some papers at him. 'This is my movement order. The highest priority.'

Another bomb exploded dangerously close. Shaw stepped smartly away from the front of the hotel.

'I should move to the middle of the road, sir. It'll be safer.'

'One hell of a mess,' the officer said, looking round.

'Aye,' Shaw said, trying to make sense of the papers. 'What's all this paperwork for?'

The officer said, 'I have to get a very important consignment to Liverpool before morning. That is a movement order. Thought you would want to check it. Security and all that.'

'Oh yes?' Shaw said irritably. 'Well, Captain. Don't you think I've got enough on?'

'Look at the signature at the bottom, Constable.'

Shaw shone his torch on the document. He read: 'Pier 16, Liverpool docks, the SS *Bellamy*, two sealed wooden cases to be delivered by 15 December by order of W.S. Churchill, Prime Minister. 13 December 1940.'

His eyes bounced when he read the signature and the typewritten name underneath.

'It's a very important consignment,' the officer said. 'For the war effort. Can you please direct me out of here and get me on my way to Liverpool?'

Shaw coughed and stuck back his shoulders. 'Right, Captain. Of course I'll try.' He rubbed his chin and looked behind him and then in front. 'Well, the roads round here are hopeless, sir. Debris all over. Try and avoid The Moor. I know Atkinsons went up more than an hour ago. You'll not get through that way. You'd be better turning round, going down the hill, working your way along West Bar, past the Police Station and out of Sheffield on the Barnsley Road, then through to Bromersley, then over Woodhead towards Manchester. You can get to Liverpool that way.'

Another huge bomb shook the ground. It landed on C & A's, which was directly opposite the remains of the Marples Hotel. The racket was deafening. The front of the store exploded and blew out. The blast knocked the two men to the ground.

The Police Station, Bromersley, South Yorkshire, UK. Wednesday, 14 February 2007. 5.00 p.m.

'Poison, sir?' Detective Sergeant Ronald Gawber said as he screwed the cap on the little bottle. 'It's for my cough. My wife swears by it.'

Detective Inspector Angel shook his head. Gawber looked at the label on the bottle.

'Don't you know that some cough medicines contain arsenic?' Angel said. 'Doesn't it say "Shake the bottle thoroughly" and "Do not exceed the stated dose"?'

Gawber looked up from the label, his eyebrows raised. 'Yes, it does, sir. I didn't know.'

'If you're not well, Ron, you should see a doctor. Too much of that jollop could muck up your kidneys.'

'It's only cough medicine, sir,' he said, stuffing the little bottle back in his pocket.

'Have you already forgotten Paracelsus's maxim?' Angel said impatiently.

Gawber's mouth dropped open. 'What's that, sir?' he said.

'Paracelsus's maxim? You should remember that, Ron. Every doctor, forensic wallah and detective, who regularly investigates murder cases, must know what Paracelsus's maxim is.'

Gawber shook his head.

Angel wrinkled his nose. 'Well,' he said slowly. 'Read, note, learn and inwardly digest, Paracelsus's maxim says that the only difference between a medicine and a poison is the dose.'

There was a moment's hesitation, then Gawber said, 'Point taken, sir, but I'll be all right. I won't take too much. I only take a little sip now and then to stop me coughing.'

Angel looked at him impatiently and shook his head.

'It's nothing, sir,' Gawber said. 'I always get a bit of a cough and a cold at this time of the year.'

'Right, lad. Be careful. That's all I wanted to say on the matter.' He turned to the door. 'I'm off for my tea.'

Gawber quickly said, 'You were telling me about the difficulties in catching and securing a conviction against a murderer.'

Although Gawber had been on Angel's team for eight years, and had observed at first hand some of his remarkable deductions, he had never discovered how the great man actually functioned. He was eager not to miss hearing anything useful he might want to say.

'Was I?' Angel said, turning back. 'I think all I was saying, Ron, was that catching a murderer is never easy, and that you might have to use subterfuge. That's all.'

Oh,' he replied. 'What do you mean exactly, sir? What sort of subterfuge?'

'It depends. Subtlety. Craft. Guile. You might not be able to solve a case by means of straightforward police work.'

Gawber said, 'Oh? Can you give me an example, sir?'

Angel wrinkled his nose and rubbed his chin. 'Well, suppose you had a tapeworm.'

Gawber's mouth dropped open again. 'A tapeworm?'

'Aye. You couldn't catch *that* by a process of question and answer and then deduction, could you? Why, you can't even see it. A slimy thing, a tapeworm. Close to you, inside you, but out of sight. You can't see it, but you know it's there. Elusive. Eating your food. Threatening your life. Just like a murderer. It has to be caught. And dealt with.'

Gawber stared at him.

'Here's what you might do,' Angel continued. 'You might go down to a sweet shop and buy a lollipop.'

'A lollipop? What sort of a lollipop?'

'Any sort. It must be on a stick, that's essential. Then put yourself on a diet. Stop eating. Just live on water. It won't do you any harm, if you're in good health. In that way, you are starving the tapeworm … starving it, you see? After three days, take the lollipop and stick it up your backside.'

Gawber gawped at him. 'Up your backside?'

'The tapeworm will be *that* hungry,' Angel said. 'It will come out for it. Then you have got him!' he added waving his hand triumphantly.

Gawber looked perplexed.

'I tell you this because I want you to be subtle and patient and adaptable, Ron. Adopt whatever means you need to solve the crime. Catch the criminal. Get him sentenced. Clean up the streets. Solving the crime is the thing. That's what we coppers in CID are about. Solving the crime. Don't let anyone else tell you any different. Form filling and fannying around with minor parking offences is for your young, brainless eager beavers. But making this town fit for ordinary decent people to live in, that's what we in CID are for. You can't always catch your criminal by doing *only* what the book says. You have to use whatever means or device is at your disposal.'

Gawber still looked rather vague.

Angel rubbed his chin and looked up at the green ceiling and flickering strip lighting for inspiration. 'I'm not getting through to you lad, am I?' he said, pursing his lips. Then, after a few moments, his eyes brightened. 'Did I ever tell you about that sixteenth century Chinese clockmaker?'

Gawber frowned and shook his head. 'No, sir.'

Angel smiled. 'Ah!' he continued enthusiastically. 'Well, there was this genius, who had a white rabbit. He used the rabbit to help him to reveal his wife's paramour.'

Gawber frowned. He hadn't heard anything about a Chinese clockmaker with a crime-detecting rabbit.

'How I envy the wisdom of that Chinese man,' Angel said. 'That rabbit made history. You know how a rabbit's nose is twitching all the time, sniffing and listening. It never stops working. Never stops. Marvellous animal. Well now, our clockmaker knew his wife was being regularly bedded by a lothario in the town, but he couldn't find out which man it was. But he thought about it and thought about it, and worked out how the white rabbit could be employed to sort it out for him. So he rounded up the suspects. They all denied having anything to do with his wife, of course. He lined them up and invited them to go into a darkened room one at a time to stroke the rabbit. He told them that the rabbit would pick up the vibes and tell him which one of them was the deceiver.'

Gawber smiled.

Angel appreciated that he had his interest. 'Accordingly,' he continued, 'each man went into the darkened room for a few minutes and then came out. And the Chinese man immediately knew which one of them it was. How?'

Gawber's face turned serious. He shook his head. 'Don't know, sir.'

'Simple, when you think about it,' Angel said. 'He had sprinkled soot on the rabbit, and the man who came out with clean hands was obviously the deceiver.'

The Mortuary, Bromersley General Hospital, South Yorkshire, UK.
Thursday, 15 February 2007. 9.30 a.m.

Doctor Mac was leaning over the naked body of a man stretched out on the rubber topped examination table, partly covered with a sheet. A powerful light was suspended over the table. A microphone was hanging next to it that lead to a small recorder on an instrument table at the side.

The pathologist, in green coat and rubber gloves opened the body's eyes with his thumbs. He sighed, then with a glance up at the microphone, said, 'Body of unidentified man found under the railway arches at Bull's Foot, Wath Road, Bromersley. Aged about fifty. Two gunshot wounds to aorta. Clean. No other wound or abrasion. Blue eyes. He appears to have been well nurtured … Slim. Has a suntan … wearing off. Must have spent time in a warmer clime … until recently. No distinguishing marks, tattoos, jewellery, body piercing or the like. Hands, regularly manicured, I think, in the past few months. Hair … greying … well maintained.'

Mac picked up an auroscope and turned the corpse's head to one side. He squeezed the switch and the light came on. He poked it into the dead man's ear and peered through it. 'Nothing untoward in the right ear.'

He turned the head over the other side and peered into the other ear. 'Nothing untoward in the left ear.'

He straightened the corpse's head and then pulled down the jaw. The smell wasn't pleasant. He pulled away.

He reached down to the table for a pencil torch and shone it into the corpse's mouth. Something glinted. He looked more closely. He spotted something unusual. Holding the orifice open with one hand, he inserted a pair of tweezers carefully into the mouth and slowly pulled out something small and yellow. It twinkled in the light. It clattered loudly as he dropped it into a kidney bowl. He lifted the bowl up to the light, then, after a few seconds, glanced up at the microphone. He was about to speak when there was a knock at the glass door behind him.

He pulled a face. He didn't like interruptions in the middle of a post mortem. He banged the dish down on the instrument table and switched off the tape recorder.

'Yes?' he called, and a young woman in a white coat opened the door. Standing next to her, was Detective Inspector Michael Angel.

'Just passing, Mac. Wanted to know how you were getting along.'

Mac licked his lips and said, 'You'd better come in, Michael.'

The young lady turned away.

Angel called after her, 'Thank you, miss.'

Without looking back, she waved an acknowledgement.

Angel strode into the examination theatre and took in the corpse on the table in front of him. 'That the tramp character?'

Mac nodded.

Angel wrinkled his nose. He had seen hundreds of bodies in the course of his work as a policeman, but the sight of another always filled him with sadness. He had expected to become used to it, but he never had. And sadly, he rarely saw a natural death.

He sniffed.

'Just started the visual. SOCO any help?' Mac said.

'No. A load of inconsistencies. Wearing tramp's conventional clobber, mucky cheap suit, well-worn and torn, but expensive, handmade shoes, and silk underwear. Had very little in the pockets. Nothing helpful. No cash. No ID.'

Mac nodded. 'I can confirm that this chap hadn't been "on the road" long.'

Angel sniffed again.

'Whatever motivates people to take up that sort of existence?' Mac said.

Angel shook his head.

Mac handed Angel the kidney bowl. 'And I have just taken *that* out of his mouth!'

Angel looked down at it and frowned. He could read a date. It said 1888 and had Queen Victoria's head clearly stamped on it. He looked up at the doctor and then back into the kidney bowl. 'Good heavens, Mac. It's a gold sovereign.'

TWO

30 Park Street, Forest Hill Estate, Bromersley, South Yorkshire, UK.
Friday, 16 February 2007. 8.00 a.m.

'I'm fed up with prunes and straw,' Angel grunted as he dug his spoon into the dish. 'What's happened to dear old bacon and egg?'

'Good for you. Starts the day properly,' Mary said. 'It's that healthy Muesli stuff,' she continued, without looking up from the local newspaper, the *Bromersley Chronicle*, which had only been delivered that morning. 'It's from Sweden.'

The bright yellow packet was on the table. He promptly reached out for it and read some of the blurb. 'It says it's made in sunny Slough.'

'Norway then,' she replied still reading.

Angel looked at her and frowned. Geography wasn't her strong point. 'Is it?' he growled slamming the packet down on the table. 'Wherever it's from, I don't want to deprive them of it.'

She suddenly whooped and pointed at the paper. 'You're mentioned here again.'

'What?'

'Yes. Just a paragraph. It's headed, "Top Detective to Solve Sovereign Murder," and goes on to say: "DI Angel is investigating the murder of an unidentified man found under Wath Road railway arches on Wednesday. He had been stabbed. An unusual feature of the death was that the man was found to be in possession of a gold sovereign."'

Angel grunted.

Mary smiled. 'Top detective, eh?'

He wrinkled his nose. 'Aye,' he said, taking a thoughtful sip of tea. 'It doesn't say that that's *all* the man had on him.'

'A sovereign in his pocket?'

'In his mouth,' he said, putting down the teacup.

'His mouth? Really?' she said. 'Like the Greeks used to do.'

'What?'

'Greek mythology.'

'Never heard of that.'

'Greek mythology! When a Greek died, he had to be taken across the River Styx, which was the sort of border between life and death, by the boatman to Hades. And the boatman had to be bribed. So the Greeks used to put coins in the mouths of their dead ones so that they could be taken across the Styx. Otherwise the ghostly remains of the dead would congregate on the nearside of the river for ever.'

'Mmm. A rum story, that.'

She resumed reading the paper. He bit into his toast.

There was a pause then she said, 'The council have closed down the Bransby Art Gallery. Been there a 122 years. Disgraceful.'

'Why?'

'Lack of support. Save money.'

'Well, if it's to save the cost of the rates …'

'It's our heritage they're closing. It was a gift to the borough. The council have no right.'

'I've never been in the place. What was in there?'

'I have. Many times. When I was young. Paintings, sculptures, works of art ... another bit of old Bromersley comes to an end.'

She resumed reading the paper. He continued attacking the toast.

Then she said, 'Guess who was in Tunistone, visiting an old farm on the moors earlier this week?'

'Don't know, do I?' he muttered through the crumbs.

'Famous film star,' Mary said excitedly. 'Eighty-four years old. Doesn't look it. Mmm. There's a photograph of her.' She held the paper up for him to see.

He glanced, then carried on munching. 'Who is it? Don't recognize her,' he said.

'It's Eloise Poole!'

'Oh,' he said. He was genuinely surprised. He certainly remembered the legendary actress. He had seen her in many films over the years. Thirty years ago, she was never off the screen or out of the news. He thought about her, remembered her in films playing opposite her husband. Well, several times with several different husbands. Now *there* was a legend! She wasn't a twopenny ha'penny lass who had appeared for a week as a bit part in a popular TV soap and was then paraded as a 'famous' actress in all the talk shows, quizzes and 'eating bugs in a jungle' show. Not that he knew any of them; he didn't watch any of the soaps.

'Any more tea? I'm going to be late.'

'Plenty in the pot. Help yourself. Listen,' she said and settled down to read it out to him.

Eloise Poole, 84, world famous film star was in Tunistone, Bromersley on Tuesday last, to see the house where her legendary father Edgar Poole was born. She was accompanied by her publicity agent, her secretary and her hair stylist. She was flown into Leeds/Bradford airport and thence in a chauffeur driven limousine the eighteen miles to the farmhouse in Tunistone, where her famous father was born in 1892 and where some of the exteriors for the film of the biography of her great, late father, Edgar Poole are to be shot. She stayed there forty-five minutes, where she met Mr and Mrs Hague, who currently live there, presented them with a miniature silver replica of Miss Poole's last Oscar for her part in *Breath In The Dark*, enjoyed a cup of tea then was driven back to the airport to fly down to London, where she stayed two nights at the Dorchester before flying back to her home on the west coast of the US. The new biopic is to star Otis Stroom and Nanette Quadrette and will take two years to make at the Euromagna Studio in Buckinghamshire and is budgeted for 28 million dollars.

Mary lowered the paper. 'What do you think to that?'

Angel lowered the teacup onto the saucer and wrinkled his nose. 'Yeah. Great stuff,' he said uninterestedly. 'Look at the time. I must be off.'

She turned the paper over and picked up a ballpoint pen. 'Before you go. Must ask you. What's the capital of Turkey?'

Angel stared at her. 'Turkey?'

'It's a competition … to win a holiday for two in Ethiopia.'

Angel shook his head. He didn't want to go to Ethiopia. 'Ankara,' he said.

'Ah,' she beamed. '*That* fits!'

'Of course it fits!'

Hague's Farm, Tunistone, Bromersley, South Yorkshire, UK. Monday, 19 February 2007. 9.00 a.m.

The Hague's farmhouse was up a narrow steep hill off the main road, five miles from Bromersley and about one mile from the tiny market village of Tunistone, on the east slope of the Pennines.

And all hell was let loose that winter's morning.

Euromagna of Hollywood and London were there to make a film. A very expensive film. They were at that site to shoot exteriors and establishing shots and the unit expected to be there about six days. For this purpose, the outside of the farmhouse had been transformed. It had been sprayed with a mud-coloured wash; the flower baskets and the plants around the doorway had been removed and replaced with plastic grass and weeds to represent less prosperous times. Powerful electric arc lamps shone onto the farmhouse with mirrors being held by young men to reflect even more light onto the scene.

A small carriage with liveried driver in Victorian gear, who was patiently holding back a jet-black horse, was positioned at the end of the lane waiting for a later scene. The horse was acting up. It was as unhappy as everybody else to be hanging around.

Vans, cars, a coach, mobile canteen and caravans of all shapes and sizes were parked higgledy-piggledy in the top field.

A tall, smartly dressed, handsome man with a burnt sienna and red face, and stuck on sideburns, was by the farmhouse door holding a well-thumbed, three-inch thick script in a plastic binding. He was smiling, and standing as though a broom handle had been inserted up his backside all the way up to his neck. That was Otis Stroom, probably the world's highest-paid actor.

Next to him was Nanette Quadrette, looking as desirable as a nose job, a boob job, three thousand pounds worth of dental work, a wig made from hair bought from six Indian girls and a two million-pound contract can make a girl. She was also just about the world's highest-paid actress.

Twenty-eight other employees – technicians, make-up people, costume people, sound engineers, stand-by electricians, carpenters and painters, gofers, continuity experts and more – all on the Euromagna payroll were standing around the two actors.

A scruffy man in jeans, T-shirt and trainers was sitting in a canvas chair, holding an electric megaphone, waving his arms around, and dishing out instructions to all and sundry. That was Mark Johannson. And he was one of the highest-paid film directors in the business.

'All right, everybody,' he bawled impatiently. 'Let's get on with it. Now, listen up. This scene leads up to when Edgar proposes to Cora. We gotta have pathos, we gotta have desire, we've gotta have lust. She comes through the yard to the door, there are words of passion at the door and then she enters. All right?' He looked across at Stroom and said, 'You need to be inside the house, Otis, and when she knocks, you answer the door and go on from there. Just as we rehearsed. OK?'

Otis Stroom smiled confidently, displaying most of his thirty-two laminated ivories, nodded, waved in acknowledgement and went into the farmhouse and closed the door.

Johannson turned to the floor manager, Sean Tattersall, and grunted, 'Right. Let's go.'

The floor manager yelled, 'Quiet everybody. Places please. Going for a take. Roll them.'

There was nervous shuffling, then stillness and silence. Even the wind stopped blowing and whistling.

A camera on a dolly was pointing at the farmhouse door. On the seat was a man with an oriental face. That was Harry Lee, well-known film cameraman, peering at the viewfinder. He said, 'Running.'

Sean Tattersall said, 'Mark it.'

A young man in a jockey cap worn the wrong way round appeared from out of the cluster of stand-by technicians and workers. He held up an illuminated marker board and shouted, 'Edgar Poole Biography. Scene twenty-one. Take one.' Then he dissolved back into the crew.

'Action,' Johannson bawled.

Quadrette, looking as desirable as a hot bacon sandwich on this cold February morning, teetered along the cobblestones four or five yards along the frontage of the farmhouse.

Harry Lee made a signal to a young man to push the camera dolly forward to follow the track of the actress.

A youth holding the sound boom followed her to catch the delicate click of her shoes on the cobblestones.

A man with a whistle warbler faced the sound boom and made the sound of a bird.

Quadrette reached the gate, went up the step and tapped on the door.

Then suddenly Harry Lee pulled his head back from the viewfinder on the camera, looked at the director and said, 'The mike's in the frame, Mark.'

Tattersall heard him and bawled, 'Cut!'

Johannson who had been following the action with one eye on the scene and one eye on the video monitor suddenly screamed out to the youth carrying the sound boom, 'The mike's in the frame, you idiot! The mike's in the frame!'

The young lad's face blushed and his pulse raced.

'You have to watch the monitor as well as the action, son,' Tattersall said.

'Can't see the monitor from here,' the young man replied.

'Well, watch the bloody camera then,' Johannson snapped. 'It's big enough, isn't it? You can see *that*, can't you? You can see the direction it's pointing?' He ran a shaky hand through his hair. 'What's your name?'

The lad looked down at his trainers. He had some thoughts about murder, but sulkily replied, 'Tim Gallagher.'

'What?' Johannson yelled. 'Speak up, boy.'

'Tim Gallagher, sir,' he said loudly, through curled lips.

Johannson sighed, then he yelled, 'There's a dozen lads here, who can hold a mike on a pole. If you can't do it right, leave it and I'll get someone who can. Understand?'

There was a pause.

'Yes,' Gallagher said, indifferently.

'Starting positions,' Johannson growled.

'Starting positions, everybody,' Tattersall echoed.

Nanette Quadrette's petite nose quivered with distaste. She moved away from the door and retraced her steps along the cobblestones. A woman rushed up and dabbed her nose with a powder puff as she turned and waited.

'Quiet everybody. Going for another take. Roll them.'

There was shuffling again, then stillness and silence.

Harry Lee said, 'Running.'

Tattersall said, 'Mark it.'

The marker boy came forward, held up the board and cried out, 'Edgar Poole Biography. Scene twenty-one. Take two.'

'Action,' Johannson bawled.

Once again, Quadrette teetered along the cobblestones towards the farmhouse door.

The camera followed her, as did the youth holding the sound boom.

The whistle warbler stepped forward and made the sound of a bird.

The scene looked and sounded good.

Johannson followed the action on the video monitor and nodded agreeably as he saw the videotape coil into the can.

Then there was suddenly the neighing of a horse and the short clatter of hooves on the cobblestones. The carriage rattled as it moved a few inches and then stopped. It came from the long-suffering horse at the end of the lane. The driver pulled tight the rein and cried, 'Whoah. Whoah there, Betsy.'

Johannson's head swivelled round to face him; his eyes shone like a wild cat caught in headlights.

The sound man pulled a face, held an earphone away from his ear and said, 'It's no good.'

Johannson's top lip tightened back against his teeth. His fists tightened causing his nails to cut into the palms of his hands.

'Cut,' he bawled, his face scarlet with rage. 'Shoot that bloody horse or put a gag in its mouth. If you can't keep it quiet, you'll be off this film and every other Euromagna production for the next hundred years. Do you understand?'

The driver looked mortified. He too coloured up red. His was with embarrassment, not rage. 'Yes, sir,' he said. 'Very sorry, sir.'

Johannson waggled a finger to summon a young man from the crew standing in the group nearby. He whispered in his ear. The gofer ran off.

Nanette Quadrette glared at Johannson, hoisted up her bosom and tightened her mouth. Johannson didn't notice. A woman rushed up with a powder puff and touched her nose again.

The gofer returned with a small bottle. Johannson took it, unscrewed the top, poured some pills into his hand, then up to his mouth and swilled them down with something from a paper cup in front of him. He sighed, ran a hand through his hair and said, 'Right, Sean.'

They began the routine all over again.

This time, everything went well. The marker boy marked the scene. The bird warbler was spot on cue.

Nanette Quadrette did her bit down the cobblestones in that long thin, tight dress, with everybody's eyes on her. She looked terrific. She was magnetic. The scene showed great promise. She seductively knocked on the door, looking desirable and full of anticipation, and waited.

The door didn't open.

She held the tension magnificently.

Johannson stared across the garden gate at it. It still didn't open.

Everybody waited. *And* waited. It was too long. The spell was broken.

Quadrette took in a deep breath, turned round, glared at Johannson, hoisted her skirt and squawked, 'Well, where the bleeding hell is he?'

Most of the crew blinked and sucked in air.

'Cut,' Johannson said through clenched teeth.

You could have cut the air with a chain saw. Everybody wondered what was going to happen next and stared at the director.

Johannson glared back at Nanette Quadette. 'I am not his nanny!' he bawled. 'This is supposed to be a professional outfit. I am dealing with a bunch of bloody amateurs!'

Then the farmhouse door opened uncertainly and the dark bronzed head of Otis Stroom poked through it. He was wearing spectacles now. He took them off, blinked, looked across at Johannson in surprise and said, 'I say, Mark, what's my cue to open the door?'

Johannson looked heavenward.

Nanette Quadrette screamed, pushed the woman with the powder puff out of the way and stormed off to her caravan.

THREE

Broadlawns, Yew Tree Lane, Weybridge, Surrey. Monday, 19 February 2007. 10.00 a.m.

'It's not enough,' Violet screamed. 'Nowhere near enough. It'll cost you a lot more than the deeds of this house to get shut of me, you bastard.' She viciously stubbed a cigarette out on the ashtray on the mantelpiece and then stormed angrily round the living room.

'Be reasonable, Violet,' the man said, standing up and rubbing each side of his moustache in turn.

'The crack in the pool needs twenty thousand spending on it. The drive needs repaving.'

'I can't possibly pay out for everything. Be reasonable, Violet.'

'Reasonable? What's reasonable? Who stuck by you when the coppers were climbing all over the house in that mucky porno caper you had going with that girl? If I hadn't lied for you, you'd have gone down for four years.'

'They weren't pornographic! They were artistic poses. Dammit you used to—'

She cut him off. 'She was under age and you knew it. I've built a very profitable business up for you, over the past ten years,' she said, lighting up another cigarette. 'While you've been away, living it up with Merle, playing at being Mr Respectable.'

'*We've* built a very profitable business, here,' he snorted. 'You're good at handling the girls, that's what it is.'

'I'm better than you, that's a certainty, *and* I can keep my hands off them as well, which is more than you damned well can.'

'There you go with the wise cracks again.'

'It's a fact. Merle wouldn't have stuck with you if she knew the half of it.'

She had gone too far. His face went scarlet. 'But she *doesn't* know,' he bawled. 'That's the point, you stupid bitch!'

She stared at him with eyes as cold as stilettos. 'Thanks to me,' she stormed. 'And only thanks to me. And don't you ever *dare* call me that again.'

He licked his lips. He knew he'd pay for that slip of the tongue.

'It's two million. *Cash*,' she snapped. 'And this house. And you're getting off cheap.'

He brushed a hand through his thinning hair. 'Can't be done, Violet. Simply can't be done.'

'Oh yes, it can,' she said confidently. 'One word. One phone call from me and you'll be in the brown stuff up to here,' she said, glaring at him and pointing to her own neck.

His face went the colour of chalk. He ran his hand across his mouth. He realized that she meant what she said. 'Look, there's no point in going on like this,' he said.

'Five years ago, you said you'd find a way, but you never did. You just kept putting it off and off, and now *you* want *out*. At *my* bloody age. And *you* want *out*. Huh!'

'Please, Violet. Be reasonable. If it hadn't been for *Merle's* money, we wouldn't be in the position we are today. It was *her* money that bought the very first lease on the offices, paid the insurance, the advertising, the photographers.'

'Stop snivelling,' she stormed. 'I can't *stand* you when you're snivelling.'

He began following her round the room. 'I am not snivelling!' he roared.

She stopped, turned and stared at him. 'I don't know what the hell I see in you,' she said. 'You're going bald, you can't write your name on a cheque without specs and you're useless in bed.'

He stared across at her, his eyes the colour of blood.

'This house and two million quid,' she shouted. 'And I'm not waiting for ever!'

DI Angel and Mary Angel lived three miles out of the centre of Bromersley, on the Forest Hill Estate. On the morning of Monday, 19 February, Mary Angel was coming into town on the bus to do some shopping and was sitting next to the window immediately behind the driver. The bus had to stop at some temporary traffic lights because of road works at the bottom of Creeford Road. The Northern Gas company had a van standing in the road next to a hole in the pavement surrounded by traffic cones.

As the bus stood there, Mary Angel was uniquely positioned to see up a narrow alleyway. She observed a girl on her stomach across the top of the wall, her long, thin legs hanging down. She had plenty of black hair, was wearing a raincoat, long socks and leather shoes. Mary saw her jump down to the narrow footpath, land badly and fall backwards. At the same time, something shiny dropped among the sprinkling of weeds on the edge of the path. The girl didn't seem to notice. She was more concerned with her inelegant fall. She quickly scrambled to her feet, shook her leg and then put her weight on the ankle to try it out. It seemed all right. She looked round, saw the bus and the faces at the windows, turned away and ran quickly away down the alley out of sight.

The traffic lights changed to green and the bus pulled away.

Mary wondered what the girl had been up to. The wall she had come over must have been the perimeter of the garden of the end house on Creeford Road. It was not the usual way for a visitor to leave a house. She couldn't ignore it, her husband being an inspector in the local constabulary. The girl had looked very furtive; her method of leaving the premises left Mary in no doubt that she had been up to something dishonest, and she was considering what next to do. She made a decision. She would phone her husband on her mobile and let him deal with it.

She reached into her handbag for the phone, when she noticed the bus was slowing down again. It stopped. She looked up. Apparently, it was a regular bus stop for passengers to alight only. One elderly lady was getting off. Mary suddenly decided to alight also and she leaped out of her seat and followed her down the steps. The doors swished shut, the bus pulled away and she watched it go wondering if she had done the right thing.

There was nobody around. A few cars whizzed past in both directions. She waited for her opportunity, crossed the road and walked back to the end of the alley. She looked up it and around about. There was no sign of the girl, or anybody else. She walked the few paces up the alley to the spot where she had seen the girl fall. Several tufts of grass had been pulled out of the old wall, and it had fresh scrape marks where she had caught her shoes on the way down. She looked down to where she thought something had been dropped. Sure enough in a clump of grass, there was something shining back at her. She reached down and picked it up. It was like a pair of scissors with a small box on one of the blades. She realized at once that it was a candle-snuffer. It looked very old, and being silver, she considered it might be quite valuable. She snapped it a couple of times. It seemed to be all right. She put it into her shopping bag and looked round to see if anything else had been dropped. There was nothing.

Mary walked back to the road junction, went round the corner onto Creeford Road to the first house. It was a big, detached Victorian pile with double wrought-iron black-painted gates standing wide open. She walked through the gates and along the short drive that was surrounded by dark evergreen bushes of several types. Then up four stone steps to the freshly painted black door.

There was a door knocker and a china bell-push. She stuck out a finger and pressed the bell. Nothing happened. After a short wait, she reached up for the door knocker, gave it a few bangs and then pressed the bell-push again for good measure.

There was still no reply. Looked like there was nobody at home.

She dug into her bag for her mobile and tapped in her husband's phone number. He soon answered and she told him the story about the girl coming over the wall, the finding of the candle-snuffer and her attempt to return it to the householder. He thought it needed following up promptly, so he told her to wait there and he'd be along right away.

She sighed and stuffed the mobile in her bag, and then strolled under the small parapet to see whatever there was to see in the garden.

A big car suddenly roared through the gates driven by a man in a hurry. He saw Mary Angel by the front door and was surprised. He slammed the car door and rushed up the steps.

She stared down at him. He was almost certainly the wealthy man who lived there, and she was pleased that she might be able to tell him the story, return the silver snuffer and press on with her shopping.

'Good morning,' he said pleasantly, his eyebrows raised. 'Did you want to see me?'

'Good morning,' she said. 'I do if you live here.'

'Indeed I do,' he said pulling out a bunch of keys and making for the door.

'Good. Then I can give you this. I believe it's yours.'

He turned back.

She reached into her bag, pulled out the candle-snuffer and handed it to him.

He took it from her, stared at it, gasped, turned it up and down, and then very seriously said, 'Well, thank you *very* much, but how on earth did you come by it?'

She began to tell him the events of the morning to which he listened most attentively. He was thanking her when another car came through the gate. She was relieved when the driver smiled reassuringly up at her. She acknowledged the smile with a small wave of the hand.

'You know the gentleman?' he said quickly.

She smiled. 'It's only my husband. It's all right. He's a policeman.'

The face of the man holding the candle-snuffer suddenly changed. His eyes bounced. 'Oh,' he said.

Angel got out of the car and came up the steps. 'Good morning, sir.'

The man smiled. It wasn't a great smile. Angel had seen more convivial smiles on a corpse. He knew the expression. It was the practised smile of a man who wanted to scream and run.

The man said, 'I'm afraid there's been some mistake.' He handed the candle-snuffer back to Mary. 'This isn't my property. I don't know who it belongs to. Thank you for showing it to me. Now, if you'll excuse me, I will have to be off. I have an appointment. Good morning.'

He went in the house and closed the door.

A few minutes later Angel drove the BMW up to the front of the five-storey building that had once been a wool mill. He locked the car door and glanced up at the big, old stone building. He noticed the large door in the wall on the top floor, and the metal arm and pulley that used to swivel out to function as a simple hoist to move wool and whatever else from one floor to another. He also observed that all the upper floors seemed deserted, indeed, some of the windows needed the attention of a glazier, but that the ground floor seemed to be fully occupied by a second-hand car showroom and motor repairers, a double-glazing window makers and, with a tiny frontage on the corner, an antiques dealer with a sign that showed that David Schuster was the tenant.

Angel walked up to the old-fashioned shop door and turned the knob. A bell on a spiral spring hanging from the low ceiling bounced and rang out loudly. He stepped down into the cramped, dusty little shop and looked around at the pictures and animal heads on plaques adorning the walls, the piled-up sticks of furniture, and mixture of modern and old household clobber packed and stuffed wherever it would fit. Piles of framed paintings, two crude sculptures, dusty curtains and curtain rails were piled up on one side and six ancient fire extinguishers were occupying floor space by the glass counter.

Angel sniffed and wondered if he had come to the right place.

A man in a Victorian smoking hat and scruffy suit shuffled through a bead curtain in a cloud of cigarette smoke. He smiled, put a lighted cigarette in an overfull ashtray, placed both hands on the counter, leaned over it and said, 'Now, sir. What can I do for you?'

'Are you Mr Schuster?' Angel said.

'My name is on the shop. I cannot deny it, sir. David Schuster, antiques, restoration and second-hand furniture. Also house clearances a speciality. Alas, there aren't many genuine antiques around these days. I have to diversify like most everybody else.'

Angel pointed to the curtains and the fire extinguishers. 'You certainly deal in a wide variety of … things.'

Schuster smiled. 'Yes, I must be mad. I have just cleared out the Bransby Art Gallery, which Bromersley council have closed down. These curtains, fire extinguishers and other things came with the deal. I will find a customer for everything in time, I expect. If those fire extinguishers are in your way, I will move them.'

Angel leaned down and pushed them to one side.

'Thank you,' Schuster said.

Angel straightened up. 'I have been told that you are an expert on silver.'

Schuster pursed his lips and struggled to look modest. For him, it wasn't easy. 'I know a bit about silver, sir. Yes.'

Angel opened the paper bag he had been holding, pulled out the candle-snuffer and offered it over the counter.

Schuster took it slowly from him, held it out disinterestedly, turned it over, then back again, then put it on the counter between them.

'Do you want to sell it?' he asked, nonchalantly.

Angel shook his head.

'It's not mine to sell, Mr Schuster. I am a police officer. DI Angel. This has come into my possession. I simply have to find out its value.'

'Ah,' Schuster said. 'Just a valuation you want?'

'Whatever you can tell me.'

'Right,' he said and reached up, dragged at a coiled metal contraption that looked like a snake. He pressed a switch at its neck and the snake's head lit up. Angel could see that it was an angle poise lamp.

Schuster directed the light onto the candle-snuffer, took a 10x loupe out of his pocket, set it into his eye, closed the other and then picked up the silver. He took a full minute casting his eye over it. He tested the action of the blades, then he put the piece down, switched off the light, put the loupe back into his pocket and said, 'Well, it's very old. Maybe 200 or 300 years or even more. Very unusual design. The tips of the snuffer are like a pair of hands. Cannot bring to mind what the hands represent. I'm sure it's something significant, but I can't think what. Delicately traced. It would have been done in the days when a silversmith was an artist and didn't charge by the hour. High standard of silver, but not English. Almost certainly made on the Continent. In good condition. Very much polished. Shows it came from a house with lots of servants. Probably polished every day. Not that useful. I mean, who uses candle-snuffers these days? Might be very interesting to a museum though. Hard to say. *I* wouldn't pay more than thirty pounds. Hmm. That would be *my* top price. In a classy auction house, like Flumen's, on a good day, you *might* get a bid of a hundred or even more. Now, if only it had been a pair of vine scissors. They're all the rage now, especially if they are antique.'

Angel was disappointed. 'Any idea where it might have come from?'

'Some big house on the Continent, where they regularly used candles, had plenty of servants, say during the seventeenth century.'

'Well, thank you, Mr Schuster. What do I owe you?'

'I'll put it on the slate, Inspector,' he said. 'It'll be a friendly smile and a hot cup of tea if ever you see me in the cells.'

Angel raised his head in surprise.

It was 8.28 a.m. when Angel arrived in the office. He threw off his coat, glanced at the pile of post on his desk and pulled a face. He fingered through it, opened one of the envelopes, sniffed and then cast it aside.

He picked up the phone and stabbed in a number. It was answered by Police Constable Ahmed Ahaz.

'Come in here,' Angel said.

Ahaz was a sensitive young man, only twenty years of age and was recently promoted from cadet to probationary police constable. He was courteous, obliging, enthusiastic and intelligent. He had been on Angel's team since joining as a cadet three years ago. The inspector liked him and thought he showed great promise.

'Now what about that misper?'

'Nothing, sir.

'You've searched *everywhere*?' Angel bawled.

'Yes sir,' he said. 'There's no match on the national computer, and I've been back through every issue of the *Police Gazette* for the past six months.'

'Have you tried the Salvation Army?'

Ahmed frowned. 'They're always asking *us*, sir.'

'Well, let's ask *them* for a change,' he quipped.

'Do you mean nationally, sir?'

'Start at their head office in London. But for god's sake get a move on and find out who he is, before he's recorded as "unknown", and has to go in a pauper's grave.'

Ahmed pulled a face.

Angel noticed. 'That's what happens if the body can't be identified.'

'Not very nice, sir.'

'No. Well, crack on with it, then.'

Ahmed opened the door.

'And send Ron Gawber in,' he called after him.

'Right, sir.' He went out.

Angel watched the door close. He sighed, rubbed his chin, leaned back in the swivel chair, looked up at the ceiling and squeezed the lobe of his ear between finger and thumb. He wasn't a happy bunny. He liked being a policeman, but he didn't like crime, especially not in his birth town of Bromersley, which had more than its fair share. He sighed again. Bromersley was just a big wet hole with ugly buildings and no style. Its people were mostly good-hearted except those that weren't, of which there were too many. He wanted better for the community, for his wife and for himself.

There was a knock at the door.

He lowered the chair. 'Come in.'

It was Detective Sergeant Ronald Gawber.

'You wanted me, sir?'

'Yes. That tramp. Still no ID. You were on the scene first, Ron. Tell me about it again. Sit down.'

Ron pulled out the chair by the desk. 'Got an anonymous triple nine, sir. Man's voice. Simply said there was a dead man under the railway bridge arches on Wath Road, Bromersley. When I got there the place was deserted except for that body. It was on the deck in a sitting position, head down. Looked drunk at first … until I got close up. The blood—'

'Yeah. Yeah. I saw the photos. What about the scene?'

'There was nobody there, sir. There were a few beer cans, a brandy bottle, newspapers, cigarette ends and so on. They were all gathered up, labelled by SOCO. There's sure to be prints on the stuff.'

Angel wrinkled his nose. 'Anything else?'

'I felt his neck. Stone cold. I phoned SOCO and waited until they arrived. They took over.'

'Yes. Ta. Got SOCO's report. It points out that the tramp was wearing handmade shoes. It might lead us somewhere.'

Gawber nodded. 'Anything in the pockets, sir?'

'No. Nothing.'

'Robbed, I expect. Hmm.' Gawber pulled a face like the smell in a drunk's cell on a Sunday morning, and said, 'Who could go through a dead man's pockets and take absolutely everything?'

Angel could only think of the Inland Revenue.

'Is that it, Ron?'

'Yes, sir.'

'Mmm.'

He turned to go.

'There's something else,' Angel said. 'You've heard about the man at Number 2 Creeford Road?'

Gawber smiled wryly then said, 'Oh yes, sir. The chap who couldn't decide whether that candle-snuffer was his or not.'

'Aye. I've got Crisp getting the full SP on him. But have you any idea of the thief? It was a girl, with longish dark hair, slim, wears socks, like a schoolboy.'

'Why would she wear socks like a boy?'

'How do I know?'

'You mean pulled up to just below the knee and then turned over?'

'That's the description my wife gave me.'

'I've no knowledge of a customer like that, sir. But kids wear anything these days.'

'Yes, but … a bit unusual for a girl. They always want to look … older, more sophisticated.'

'How old was she?'

Angel shrugged. 'My wife said she could have been any age from about fifteen to twenty-five.'

There was a knock at the door. It was Ahmed.

'Excuse me, sir. Got through to the Salvation Army. They're looking through their records. They'll phone back tomorrow after they've made a thorough search.'

'Right.'

He turned to go.

'Hang on a minute, Ahmed.'

Angel looked at Gawber. Gawber stood up and said, 'I'll get off, sir. I expect SOCO will be able to release those shoes by now.'

'If you've any difficulty, let me know. I'll not have our enquiries held up. And think on about that girl.'

'Yes, sir.' Gawber went out.

Angel glanced at Ahmed. 'Close the door and come and sit down,' he said. Then he reached into the bottom drawer of his desk, took out a large paper window envelope printed with the one word EVIDENCE in red, and placed it on the desk in front of him.

'Have a look at that.'

The young man opened the envelope and carefully took out the candle-snuffer. His face brightened. He turned it over and back again.

'It's very ... elegant, sir,' he said, looking at it carefully and deferentially. He ran his fingers along the delicate silver tracing, exercised the scissor movement twice and looked curiously at the moulded silver hands at the tips of the blades.

'It's for snuffing out candles, and for trimming the wick.'

Ahmed nodded.

'I want you to photograph it, put it on the stolen list on the NPC, also, I want hard copies sending to Matthew Elliott at the Antiques and Fine Art squad, the *Police Gazette* and *Antiques' World*, with this caption.' He handed Ahmed a used envelope with some handwriting on the back.

Ahmed read it out.

Silver candle-snuffer with hand motif on tips of blades. Found locally, believed stolen, thought to have been made in the 18th century on the continent. Any information to DI Angel, The Police Station, CID, Church Street, Bromersley.

FOUR

The phone rang. Angel reached out for it.

'Come down here, smartish,' the voice bawled, and the line went dead.

It was Superintendent Harker. Sounded urgent. It always did.

Angel wrinkled his nose and wondered what the panic was. Everything was going on satisfactorily in his cases ... a bit slow, maybe, but he reckoned he was making progress on all fronts.

He dashed straight down the green painted corridor to the superintendent's office, tapped on the door and went in.

'You wanted me, sir?'

'Ah,' Harker groaned and pulled a face like an orangutan in the dock awaiting the judge's sentence. He sniffed and pointed to a chair. It was the nearest Angel would ever get to a polite invitation to sit down. He eased himself into the chair facing the desk and looked across at the superintendent who was assembling four sheets of A4 in sequence before tossing them into the out tray.

He looked more miserable and mean than usual: like a crocodile that had just eaten a murderer, a housebreaker, two shoplifters and a police cadet, and was now suffering from violent indigestion. He burped, which almost made Angel smile.

Harker then reached out for a yellow sticky note directly in front of him. He looked at it and said, 'Ah. Here it is. Just come in. A triple nine. Looks like murder.'

Angel's head came up. Sounded interesting. Another challenge. His heart started banging.

'A man found dead in a caravan up at Hague's farmhouse in Tunistone,' Harker continued. 'Man called Tattersall phoned it in. I have advised SOCO and Dr Mac.' Harker passed the note to him.

Angel took it, read it, frowned and shook his head. There was never an end to murder: like painting the Forth Bridge. Unusual though, in a caravan.

'Well, get on with it,' Harker bawled.

Angel leaped up and made for the door.

'And I don't want you dragging it out. Don't make a saga of it ... like Blair's exit from Number Ten.'

Angel's lips tightened against his teeth. 'I never do, sir. I never do.'

He raced up the corridor to the CID office and bumped into Ahmed. 'Ah. I'm on a murder case up at Hague's farmhouse in Tunistone. Find Crisp and Scrivens and get them to join me there. Pronto.'

'Murder?' Ahmed muttered. He felt the hair stand up on the back of his neck. 'Right, sir,' he stammered, but Angel didn't hear him. He was nowhere to be seen. Ahmed heard the station rear door slam.

It didn't take Angel long to reach the farm in Tunistone. He knew the way. It was off the main road across the Pennines to Manchester up a single-track rough road. When he drove through the farm gate, the big hay field was like a circus ground without the big top. Cars, vans, trailers and caravans were parked in no particular formation and about thirty people were milling round in groups of two and more, several others were propping up the serving hatch of the mobile canteen drinking tea out of plastic cups. He spotted SOCO's unmarked white van and Dr Mac's car parked outside one of the three big chromium and glass American caravans. He drove across the uneven field and parked behind them. A few of the people glanced in his direction, but soon turned away when he looked directly at them.

One of the big caravans and the steps into it was already taped around with blue and white DO NOT CROSS tape. A small man in a white paper suit came down the steps carrying a bag and pulling a mask away from his mouth. It was Dr Mac. He saw Angel and came across to him.

'This one yours, Michael, I take it?'

'Aye. What you got, Mac?' Angel said to the white-haired Scot.

'One dead male. Shot in the chest. Died instantly, I think.'

'What sort of calibre?'

'Might be able to talk about that when I've had a closer look.'

'Any weapons there?'

'I didn't see any.'

'Did you get the victim's name?'

'Mark Johannson. Big noise film director, they tell me. I've never heard of him. He was the man in charge of this outfit.'

'Oh?' Angel sniffed. 'What was the time of death?'

'Hmmm. Must have been some time yesterday … late afternoon or evening.'

'Thanks, Mac. I'll ring you tomorrow.'

The doctor nodded and turned away to his car.

Angel reached into his pocket for his mobile, flicked it open and tapped in a number. Superintendent Harker answered.

'Angel, sir. I'm going to need some help up here, and quick. Looking round, there are between thirty and forty potential witnesses. I need statements taking from each one before they disappear into the undergrowth.'

'What about your own team?' he growled.

'Gawber's on that murdered tramp case, sir. Crisp and Scrivens are on their way here.'

There was a pause, then Harker said, 'I don't know where you think I can conjure men up from. I'm not Houdini. I'll get onto Asquith.' The phone went dead.

Angel pocketed the mobile and turned towards the caravan.

A young man of about twenty-five, hands in pockets, who had been hovering nearby, caught his eye and ambled up to him. 'Are you from the police?' he said tentatively.

'Yes, lad. DI Angel, Bromersley police.'

'I'm the floor manager. Sean Tattersall. I'm sort of … in charge of the unit, until someone else is appointed director.'

'Oh, yes. It was you that reported the death. You are making a film here?'

'We *were*.'

'Well, who are all these people?' Angel said. 'Actors?'

'No. They are mostly crew. There are only two actors here: Otis Stroom and Nanette Quadrette. They want to leave. Well, everybody does. Of course, I have contacted the studio and told them what's happened. They have just phoned back to say that Mr Montague is on his way up here to sort things out. He should be here shortly.'

Angel frowned. He mustn't lose any potential witnesses. 'Nobody leaves here without my say-so, Mr Tattersall. Please see to it. All right? And I want a list of everybody present.'

'Right, Inspector.'

'Thank you. Did you see what happened?'

'No. But I found him – the body.'

'Tell me about it.'

'I went in and found him on the floor. He was obviously dead. Looked as if he had been there some time. I dialled 999 on my mobile and then came back and told Miss Quadrette and Mr Stroom and the crew.'

'What made you call on him?'

'He was late. On location, we normally start shooting at eight o'clock, if the light's good. Johannson is the director.

He's usually on the set well before then. By five past, I wondered what had happened. He was never late. I came to his caravan to see where he was. I tapped on the door and called out. There was no reply.'

'Did Mr Johannson have any enemies?'

Tattersall smiled wryly. He hesitated. 'He wasn't much liked by anybody.'

'Oh?'

'He was … impatient … and anxious … had a reputation to maintain. He was in the top league of film directors, you know … won awards in the US, UK, Japan and—'

'Yes, but was there any particular person who might have wanted him dead?'

'Don't know about that,' Tattersall lied.

'When was the last time *you* saw him alive?'

'Just after we finished, yesterday afternoon. That would be about five o'clock. We lost the light at about 4.30. He called it a day. I got a gofer to ring for the cars for him, Miss Quadrette and Mr Stroom, and then he and I and Harry Lee had a look at the rushes – the scenes in the can. We'd just about done when the coach came, so I left.'

'Harry Lee?'

'He's the cameraman.'

'You went in a coach somewhere?'

'Into the town, Bromersley. I am staying at The Feathers with some of the others. Other crew members are in guest house accommodation … wherever they can get.'

'Johannson lived in here?' Angel nodded towards the caravan.

Tattersall looked mildly amused. 'No. It's a day cabin. Space of his own. Miss Quadrette and Mr Stroom have the same thing. Somewhere private to relax and rest, wash up and have a drink, have meetings, make phone calls. They've each got a suite at the Imperial Grand Hotel in Leeds. Hire cars and drivers or taxis take them back to the hotel. They don't always stay the night there. If we finish early, they may fly back to London to get a night at home. Then back up at dawn.'

Angel's eyebrows shot up. 'And what did they do last night?'

'I really don't know.'

Angel nodded thoughtfully. 'And what did you do?'

'The coach dropped me and others at The Feathers. I went to my room, had a shower, went down for a meal around seven, then came back, had an early night, watched a bit of telly in bed and was asleep by about 10.30.'

Angel scribbled something on the back of an old envelope and said, 'Thank you. Must leave it at that for now, Mr Tattersall. Must press on.' He turned towards the caravan. 'I would be obliged if you would let me have that list,' he said calling back. 'Nobody can leave. There'll be police personnel up soon to take their names and addresses and interview them.'

'Yes, of course,' Tattersall said with a wave and moved away.

Angel lifted up the tape and stepped underneath. He noticed the name: 'Mark Johannson, Director,' neatly painted in black on the door.

At that moment, the caravan door opened and out came Detective Sergeant Donald Taylor, the senior SOCO man at Bromersley. He was dressed in a white paper suit, headcover and white wellies. He saw Angel, pulled the mask down to his chin and said, 'This your case, sir?'

'Aye, Don. What have you got?'

'Nothing very helpful, I'm afraid,' he replied snapping the latex gloves as he took them off. 'The only fresh prints around the caravan appear to be his own. There are no footprints anywhere. There doesn't appear to have been a break-in. There are various things around the van that *might* have been valuable, but we can't say for certain what has been taken, if anything. Dr Mac may uncover something helpful at the post mortem, I don't know. No sign of a struggle or disturbance. No hint at what he was doing immediately prior to death. No weapons, explosives, drugs, cash, jewellery or porn at the scene. There's nothing unusual at all.'

Angel frowned.

Another man in whites appeared at the door. He was carrying two big plastic bags, a suitcase and he had a camera on a strap slung round his neck.

Angel looked up at him. 'Have you finished in there, son?'

'Yes, sir,' the constable replied.

'I can't contaminate it then?'

'The body's still there, sir,' the constable said. 'But Dr Mac has seen it.'

'Aye.' Angel sighed lightly. Forensics weren't offering anything in the way of clues. There didn't seem to be anything much to go on; he was as in the dark as ever. He turned to Taylor.

'Right, Don, let's have a look then,' he said making for the door. 'Everything as it was?'

'Had to turn the body on its back, otherwise it's the same. I have taken photographs of it face down on the carpet as we found him. And photos of surrounds, walls, furniture in different planes.'

'Right,' he said. Angel followed him into the caravan.

It was airy, with blinds open at large windows. There were heavily upholstered bench seats at each side of the area. The body of a big, blond-haired man with a fresh ruddy face and blue eyes stared up at them from the floor. A patch of congealed blood was set on his blue shirt.

Angel never liked dead bodies, especially those that had been murdered. He wrinkled his nose. Murder was such a waste.

He stood motionless by the body and breathed in slowly and evenly. Then he crouched on his hands and knees and surveyed the scene from that position. He stood up and moved across to the other side of the body, his eyes registering anything and everything. His face didn't reveal whether he had spotted anything unusual or not. He rubbed his chin, then turned away and looked into the bathroom and kitchen.

Taylor watched him closely. 'Any ideas, sir?'

FIVE

Ten minutes later, a plain black van with two attendants arrived and took the body of Mark Johannson away in a plastic body bag to Bromersley mortuary for Dr Mac to perform a post mortem in due course. Shortly after that the SOCO team packed up their bags, took off their whites and left.

Angel finished his cursory examination of the caravan and opened the door in time to see DC Edward Scrivens, PC John Weightman and WPC Leisha Baverstock arrive in two cars, which they parked behind his.

Tattersall was drinking tea outside the catering van, and seeing the police uniforms dashed across waving a sheet of paper. Angel was pleased to see the officers and introduced him to them. He then instructed them to divide the names on the list between them and interview each person in private. They were to ask whether Johannson had any particular enemies, and specifically he wanted to know the address of their accommodation while they were here at work, as most or all were away from home, as well as their usual home address. Also, most importantly, he wanted to know where each person had been between 5.00 p.m. and midnight the previous day. Ideally, the latter would need to be corroborated by at least one other person to establish any alibi.

Sean Tattersall tactfully suggested that Angel might like to interview the two actors Miss Quadrette and Mr Stroom himself, as he was finding them particularly unmanageable and were both threatening to leave the set. Angel agreed. The list was appropriately adjusted and the squad dispersed quickly to find their allocated interviewees.

Tattersall directed Angel to the two similar luxury American caravans close by and he started to cross the field to the nearest, when a big chartreuse-green car rocked noisily towards him. It was driven by a smart chauffeur dressed in a grey suit and cap. The car slowed, and through the window the driver called out, 'Inspector Angel! Inspector Angel!'

He turned. His eyebrows raised. 'Yes?'

A bulky man in a sharp, shiny blue suit slipped out of the back door of the car and came up to him, holding out his hand.

'Ah. Inspector Angel, I'm Grant Montague,' he took his hand and shook it enthusiastically. 'I'm so very pleased to meet you. I want to offer you my complete cooperation and the cooperation of Euromagna films in your investigation into this dreadful business. I am a director of the main board and I can't tell you how distressed the chairman and the other directors are at this tragedy.... The death of Mark Johannson is such a great loss to his friends and loved ones, but also to Euromagna and to the industry. As soon as I heard, I took a plane to get here as soon as ever I possibly could.'

Angel sighed. He rescued his hand before it turned into butter and said, 'Yes. Er, thank you, Mr Montague.'

'You must call me Grant. And how can I be of service to you and your investigations?'

'Did you know Mark Johannson well?'

'As well as anybody, I guess.'

'Well, do you know of anyone who might have wished him dead?'

Montague looked shocked. 'Certainly not, Inspector. The man was respected the world over. One of the best directorial talents this century. The world was at his feet. I don't know how we are going to replace him. Our lawyers are working on it as we speak. The authorities have already expressed a wish for the return of his body to Norway for interment. Naturally, Euromagna would prefer a funeral in London and would be privileged to organize and pay for such an event.'

Angel was anxious to press on with his interviews. 'Well, that's out of my control, but, in any event, there has to be a post mortem. If you will excuse me …' He turned away.

Montague was at his elbow. 'Is there any way in which I, or Euromagna can assist you, Inspector?'

'No, thank you, Mr Montague.'

'Please do call me Grant.'

'There's nothing I can think of at the moment,' Angel said.

'There must be something…?'

'No. I don't think so. If you'll excuse me.'

'Of course,' he replied, but he was still running along beside him. 'But … but, you will have no objection to the continuation of the shooting of the film, will you, Inspector? It is a vital piece of historical work, a true life love story that must be recorded and shared with the world.'

'No. I suppose not. Provided that it in no way interferes with the murder investigation.'

'Of course, Inspector. I wouldn't dream of … in any way. Of course. Thank you.'

Angel continued the short journey towards the caravan and read the name painted on the door: 'Miss Nanette Quadrette'. It was a world famous name in the entertainment business; almost in spite of himself, he was a little curious and mildly excited at meeting the famous celebrity. He couldn't hear Grant Montague anymore and therefore assumed he had given up the chase and turned back. He didn't look to find out. He tapped on the door in front of him.

It was soon answered by a young, slim man with dyed blond hair. He was wearing an open-necked white silk shirt, black velvet trousers and a pair of flip-flops. He was holding a small glass of what looked like champagne. He looked bored. He blinked and spoke with a lisp. 'Are you the poleethman?'

Angel stuck out his chest and put on his best butch voice. 'I want to see Miss Quadrette, please.'

The young man looked back over his shoulder and said, 'It's the poleethman, Nan. Do you want to speak to him?'

There was some hiatus. Angel couldn't hear or see what was going on. After a few seconds, she must have nodded or said something in agreement because the young man pulled open the door and stepped back to permit Angel access.

Angel wondered what the world famous beauty was really like to talk to. He couldn't stop himself from smiling like an immature groupie as he climbed up the steps.

Although the caravan was similar, if not identical, to Johannson's, it was much fuller: you could say, crammed. There were several vases and containers of flowers, mostly long-stemmed varieties in various parts of the sitting room area. The two settees had been opened up into a daybed and Nanette Quadrette was lying on it, in a long, white silk robe, her hair in a turban and leaning up on one elbow with a glass in her hand. Only her face, neck, hands and feet were uncovered, and were deep brown showing that she had recently been in the sun. A smile hung from her moist lips and her eyes were slightly glazed, enough for Angel to know that she was high on something … something from a needle or a bottle. As it happened, he saw an open wine bottle nestled in an ice bucket on a stand near the foot of the bed.

'Have a drink, Mr Policeman,' she said croakily, waving the glass at him and looking across at the slim young man.

Angel stared at her. He couldn't help himself. He thought her mouth the most beautiful mouth in the world, and her teeth the whitest and most perfectly matched … and her voice. He had to agree, she was stunning. Not as stunning as she was on the screen, but she had two other enormous advantages, as far as he was concerned. She was female and she was young.

He licked his lips, then breathed out a long sigh and said, 'You are very kind, but no thanks, Miss Quadrette. I must introduce myself. My name is Inspector Angel.'

'Sit down, Inspector,' she said. 'This is Hugo, my personal ... hairdresser.' She took a sip from the glass, looked at Angel and giggled.

Angel looked across at the young man and nodded.

'Pleathed to meet you, Inspector,' the man said. 'It's Hugo Moth.' Angel assumed he intended to say 'Moss'.

She puckered up her lips and said, 'Give the inspector a glass, Hugo.'

Angel waved his hand and said, 'No thanks. I'm only here to ask you about Mark Johannson.'

The smile vanished. 'Mark Johannson?' She lifted her head and wrinkled her nose. 'We all know he's dead. What do you want to know? I didn't kill him. I don't know who did. Whoever it was should be given a bloody medal. That's all I know,' she said and then she sat up, swivelled round and put her bare suntanned feet on the cream carpet.

Moss dashed across, pulled out some gold-coloured slippers from under the bed and quickly began to slip them onto her feet. She hardly seemed to notice.

'I want to get back to London,' she continued. 'They won't be shooting anything here today. I have been asked to wait here to see you, and then I'm off, like a bat out of hell.'

'I'm coming with you, Nan?' Moss said in a beseeching tone, looking up from the kneeling position, pushing a slipper onto her foot.

She smiled down at him. 'Of course you are, Hugo dear,' she said, running her hand through his blond hair and pulling his head into her bosom with her free hand.

Moss reached out with both hands and caressed her waist with movements of a dying butterfly.

Angel watched them. The magic left him, and he decided he'd never touch Sherry trifle with double cream and chocolate sauce again.

After a few moments, she smiled down at Moss and said, 'Phone for a car to the airport, Hugo, darling ... and tell them, half an hour.'

He nodded, smiled and pulled away.

Angel then said, 'I take it you didn't like Mr Johannson.'

Her face straightened. The smile vanished again. The mood changed again. 'Horrible man. No manners. No understanding of artistic interpretation. A bully. Conceited. A liar and a cheat. And he had absolutely no idea how to treat a lady. Inspector Angel, if I had known that he was to direct this film, I would not have committed myself to Euromagna. Do you know, I turned down a million pounds to play opposite Kirk Fletcher with Maximillia Films, and had already planned to have a year away from the camera, but smarmy Grant Montague suckered me into this ... this so-called extravaganza, which was going to beat all box office records *ever*. Directed by the *great* Mark Johannson. Look at the damned film now! They'll probably never finish it. It's jinxed.'

Angel had been watching her carefully. She spoke about Johannson with expressionless eyes, cold eyes; eyes, he considered, that could watch a lion tear the innards out of a man and be unmoved. He shook his head to get rid of the imagery.

Moss closed up the mobile phone he had been talking into and said, 'Nan, the car will be here in half an hour. There's a plane at 12.32.'

She heard him and nodded but her mind was elsewhere.

'When did you last see Mr Johannson?' Angel said.

'Last night. After we had finished shooting,' she said draining the glass and offering it to Moss. He took it and reached back to take the bottle out of the ice bucket. Quadrette rocked her hand and shook her head to indicate that she didn't want any more. He put her glass down, lifted the bottle and poured the last few dregs into his own glass then pushed the empty bottle upside down into the ice bucket.

'Tell me about it,' Angel said.

'Oh. Yesterday was dreadful. There was an annoying take. The first take of the morning. We never recovered from it. It was a perfectly dreadful start to a most irritating day. That clown, Otis Stroom, hadn't learned the bloody script. He didn't know his lines or his cues. He's as blind as a bat, you know. And he can't use idiot boards because he can't see them. Playing opposite him is hard work, I can tell you. When the light went and Mark Johannson called it a day, I wasn't sorry. I came back here. Wardrobe undressed me and took my costume. I just had time to put on my robe, when he knocked on the door. I wasn't pleased to see him. And I let him know it. He came in all apologetic. I told him that I had a good mind to walk out but he pleaded with me to stay. He said it would get better, that he was going to speak to Otis Stroom and make certain he was briefed for tomorrow's schedule. I told him that I had psyched myself for the scene and the kissing business at the door seven times, and when it came to the eighth take, I was not at my best. He said that he and Harry Lee had seen the playback and that they both agreed it was marvellous and couldn't be bettered by anybody.' She waited for Angel to look impressed: he didn't oblige.

'Did anything else happen?'

'No. He left after that and I got dressed. I wanted the hell out of it. My car was due any moment.'

'Was anybody here with you at the time?'

'No. Just the two of us.'

'What happened then?'

'My car arrived. I left for my hotel in Leeds, where I spent the night.'

'What time was that?'

'I arrived in my suite at the Imperial Grand at around 5.45, I think. Had a long bath. A meal in my room … perfectly dreadful. Went through the script for today's scenes. Hugo dropped in to check my hair.' She looked across at him and smiled. 'Didn't you, darling?' she called, gesticulating with her arm.

Moss looked gooey-eyed at her. Then crossed to her and took her hand.

Angel thought the lad had better watch out later. The first sign of anything wrong and she'd bite off his arms and stuff them down his throat.

'What time was that?'

She looked at Moss.

He said, 'Just after thix o'clock, it would be.'

'Where were you until then, Mr Moss?'

'I have my own thalon in Leeds, Inspector. I was there all day until 5.30. I went thraight to the hotel. I arrived just after thix o'clock,' he said looking at Quadrette for verification.

'Yes,' she said. 'That's about right.'

'And what time did he leave?'

She frowned. Her thin, mean, sexy lips tightened. 'Are these questions really necessary, Inspector?'

He pursed his lips. 'It's simply to establish an alibi for you.'

Her eyes lit up briefly. She seemed taken aback. 'Do you think I need one?' she said in a low, growling voice.

He shrugged. 'At this stage in the investigation, I don't know.'

'The text of this interview will *not* be made available to the press, will it?'

'No. This is entirely a police matter. I am simply trying to discover the murderer of Mark Johannson. I don't have any other interest, I assure you.'

She wrinkled her nose. 'Very well, Inspector,' she said. 'Yes. Hugo was here all night. He left after breakfast.'

Angel turned back to him. 'Is that right, sir?'

Moss smirked and said, 'Yeth.'

Angel completed the interview by asking Quadrette and Moss their respective addresses. He noted the information on an envelope from his inside pocket, thanked them and made for the caravan door.

Angel immediately noticed that the air outside smelled fresher. Much fresher. He breathed in deeply and enjoyed it.

He was thinking about the heavy, warm smell in Quadrette's van. The bouquet from the flowers, her perfume and Moss's hair lacquer was a rich mixture indeed. Probably rich enough to run a Porsche for a week.

He strode determinedly to the next caravan to see Otis Stroom. As he knocked on the door, out of the corner of his eye, he saw Grant Montague strutting up to Quadrette's van followed by the chauffeur who was carrying a huge bouquet of flowers. Angel wondered what sort of a welcome Quadrette would give him. He would have loved to have had a bug planted in there and be able to overhear their conversation.

The door of the caravan was opened by the great film star himself, Otis Stroom. Angel could not avoid experiencing a brief tingle of inexplicable pleasure as he stood in front of the six foot two, tanned, muscular film idol, who was wearing a robe made from towelling material and leather slippers. There was more skin than hair on his forehead and crown, than was seen in his films, and he was also wearing a pair of bottle bottom spectacles.

'Mr Stroom,' he said with a smile. 'Detective Inspector Angel.'

'Ah, yes. I have been expecting you. Come in, Inspector. Dreadful business. Please sit down. How can I assist you?'

The men each sat on a settee at opposite sides of the caravan facing each other, with a small folding table between them. The room was uncluttered, clean and tidy.

'For the time being, Mr Stroom, by simply answering a few questions, that's all.'

'Fire away.'

'Well, firstly, do you know of anybody who disliked Mark Johannson?'

Stroom rubbed his big square chin three or four times. He didn't seem to be in any hurry. 'Well, to tell the truth, he didn't have the most attractive personality. He was a man totally lacking in personal charm. He had perfected the art of rubbing everybody up the wrong way.'

'Do you know anybody who hated him enough to *murder* him?'

'Oh no. I wouldn't go that far.'

'Nobody in particular comes to mind?'

'No. Sorry, Inspector.'

Angel nodded thoughtfully. 'Your relationship with him was good, then?'

'On the contrary. To tell the truth, I couldn't abide the man, but he was the director, the boss and he was a company man. He thought he knew all the answers. He always thought that his interpretation of a storyline was the correct and only one. He was sometimes quite amateurish, I thought, when it came to artistic interpretation. Also, we had constant arguments about angle of shot. You see, I can only show the camera my left profile. It is so much better than my right. So, I very reasonably insist, I believe, on being to the left of my co-star, which didn't always suit his choreography. You will understand that I do have a responsibility to my public. I must make the very best of myself, at all times. They must always see me looking at my best, and my female fans in particular, must not be let down. Also, some men model themselves on me. I mustn't let them down either.'

Angel screwed up his face. He was about to ask him for some clarification, but decided not to bother. Instead he moved on. 'Yes, well, where were you between five o'clock yesterday and midnight?'

'What you mean, Inspector, is, do I have an alibi?'

Angel nodded.

Stroom rubbed his big, square chin again. 'After finishing shooting yesterday, Mark Johannson came here and we had a few words about the day's shooting. It had not gone well. Everybody's nerves were shot. I understand that Harry Lee's first take had been messed up. Then Nanette Quadrette could not get a simple bit of business right, and she didn't even have any words to remember! Seven times she went through the simple matter of walking down a path to the farmhouse door and knocking on it. It was only on the eighth take that she managed to get it right.'

'What did Johannson want?'

'Oh. To make peace with me, I think. He was not hitting it off with her. He couldn't do with being at odds with both of us at the same time,' he said with a grim smile.

'And what time did he leave?'

'About five o'clock. Could have been a few minutes before that.'

'Had he stayed long?'

'No. About five minutes.'

'He left perfectly all right?'

'I wouldn't say that, Inspector. He was angry. So was I.'

'Where did he go after he left you?'

'I don't know. My car arrived about then. I rushed to get dressed. Then I was driven to my hotel, the Grand Imperial in Leeds.'

'Did you stay in the hotel all night?'

'No. I was bored and I was restless. I put on some jeans, an old coat and hat so that I wouldn't be recognized, and went out for a walk. Walked round looking in shop windows and restaurant frontages. Must have meandered for two or three hours. Found a quick service restaurant. Had a meal. Don't know where it was. Then saw a taxi, flagged it down and told the driver to take me back to the Grand Imperial.'

'What time was that?'

Stroom rubbed the big chin again. 'About eleven, I think. The lobby in the hotel was deserted.'

'You picked up your room key?'

'No need. I had it on me. I had not handed it in.'

'You spoke to nobody in all this time. Nobody recognized you?'

'No.'

Angel sniffed. 'It isn't an alibi, Mr Stroom. Your whereabouts cannot be accounted for or supported by anybody else.'

'No. Well, no matter, Inspector. You're not likely to be accusing me of murdering Mark Johannson.'

'I hope not,' Angel said, rubbing his own chin. 'I hope not.'

SIX

'You're back, sir,' Ahmed said. He seemed relieved and followed him into his office.

Angel looked at him curiously. 'Everything all right, lad?'

'There have been a couple of phone calls for you, sir.'

'Oh?' Angel said. 'Who from?'

'They were both from a man called Peter.'

'Peter who?'

'He didn't say, sir. He said he'd ring back.'

Angel sniffed. 'Hmm. Is DS Crisp in the CID room?'

'No, sir.'

'Find him for me. Smartish. He's always hard to find, that lad. I don't know where he gets to.'

Ahmed went out and closed the office door.

Angel looked down at the pile of papers in front of him. The phone rang. It was Gawber.

'We've finished here, sir. I'm sending the others back to the station. Do you want me to go over Johannson's caravan?'

'I've done that, Ron. No harm in you having a look, though. Get the feel of the scene. Then I want you to go over to the Grand Imperial Hotel in Leeds. Take young Scrivens with you. Johannson was staying there. SOCO should have been and gone by the time you get there. Have a look round. Go through his stuff. Pack it up and bring it back here. And check at the hotel on his phone calls and any messages he might have been left.'

'Right, sir.'

'Have you seen Trevor Crisp on your travels?'

'No, sir. Wasn't he looking into the ID of that man who you thought had been burgled by that girl?'

'Aye, he was,' he grunted through gritted teeth.

'If I see him, sir, I'll tell him you want him.'

'Right,' Angel said and banged down the phone. Crisp always annoyed him. He could never find him. He was always missing. He was so different from Gawber. He was always bunking off on some skive or other and eventually came back with more inventive excuses than Richard Branson.

The phone rang again. It was the civilian switchboard operator.

'There's a man wants to speak to you, sir. Been trying to get hold of you, all morning. He's phoned three times in the past hour. Says his name is Peter. That's all he'll say.'

'Oh yes? Right. I'll speak to him. Please put him through.'

There was a click.

'Hello. This is DI Angel. Who is that?'

'You don't know me, Inspector,' the voice said. 'My name is Peter Meissen. I'll come straight to the point. I understand you have in your possession an antique silver candle-snuffer with the tips of the blades in the form of a pair of hands?' The man spoke slowly; every consonant was pronounced clearly and crisply, like a man whose first language wasn't English.

'I may have.'

'Ah. Then perhaps I could see it?'

'What for? Who are you?'

'I might be prepared to make an offer to buy it for up to, say £5000.'

Angel blinked. Five thousand? That was a lot of cabbage for a silver candle-snuffer. What was so special about it? He needed to know who this man was.

'I would need to know more about your identity, sir. We don't play pig in a poke here, you know.'

'I understand that, sir. That's no problem. I can supply that when we meet, if that is satisfactory?'

'Very well,' Angel said.

The man said, 'Although you have possession of it, Inspector, do I understand that it is not actually police property?'

'That is correct. Technically, it isn't,' Angel said.

'Hmmm. Well, even so, perhaps I could call into the station this afternoon at about three o'clock?'

'Very well. I can make that convenient.'

'Good afternoon, Inspector.' He rang off.

Strange. Angel wrinkled his nose. Being a copper was a funny business. And the people he met in the course of his work were so strange. Generally, he thought, you get three sorts. You have to separate the crooks from the fools, and the fools from the innocents. Then lock up the crooks, scare off the fools and steer the innocents gently out of harm's way.

He went back to thinking about the money – £5000. That'd keep a crook in Strangeways for about eight weeks.

He looked up at the clock. It was 1.55 p.m. He was thirsty and he'd had no lunch. He reckoned that if he didn't dawdle, he would have time to trot down to The Fat Duck, grab a meat pie and a glass of Old Peculier, maybe two, and easily get back for three o'clock. It would get him out of the office and have the additional merit – maybe – of that certain solitude he needed to think things through.

It didn't take long. Only a five minute walk. There weren't many people in the pub. He found himself standing at the bar, on his own, munching through a meat pie and recalling the dead man's deep blue staring eyes and red face.

A man coughed. Angel lifted his head. At the same time the landlord placed a second glass of his favourite real ale in front of him. Angel looked up at the landlord, who pointed to a very tall man who was standing at the bar next to him.

'Inspector Angel?' the man said.

Angel looked at the glass. Picked it up, looked at the man, and said, 'For me?'

The man nodded.

'Well, thank you,' Angel said. He smiled, put the glass down and said, 'What's it going to cost me?'

The man smiled. 'Information sir. That's all.'

Angel didn't recognize him. He looked very respectable. He was big, well dressed, suit, collar, tie and polished leather shoes. No specs. No moustache. Businessman, professional man or salesman. He would certainly remember him from now on.

'I understand you've come across an old silver candle-snuffer.'

Angel was surprised, but he didn't show it. He took another modest bite of the pie. Chewing it would give him a bit of thinking time. There was something going on and he wanted to know what it was. There were too many enquiries about the thing. 'I might have. How do you know about it?'

'We have our ways, Inspector. We have our ways.'

'And who are you, anyway?'

'Just a humble newspaperman trying to earn an honest crust. George Fryer.'

Angel took another bite of the pie. He chewed it for a few seconds then said, 'What paper are you with, Mr Fryer?'

'I'm freelance.'

'Oh? Where's your press card?'

'Ah. I haven't got it on me.'

'Show me some ID then.'

'Certainly. My passport, driving licence and credit cards and everything are in the car. Excuse me just a minute, I'll get them.' He smiled and went out through the swing door.

Angel nodded after him and immediately walked over to the window at the other side of the saloon bar. He took out his pen, clicked it ready and then he pulled out an envelope from his inside jacket pocket. He then gazed out of the window. A smart, silver Volkswagen Jetta whizzed past the window. It had to slow down at the car park exit. Long enough for Angel to read the number plate. He wrote it down on the envelope, then pocketed the pen and envelope, returned to the bar, finished the pie and emptied his glass. He left the other full glass, untouched and walked out of the pub.

'Ahmed!'

PC Ahaz dashed over from his desk to the door of the CID room.

'Ahmed,' Angel said holding out a torn scrap of paper. 'Tap out the owner of this car. Here's the number. It's a silver Volkswagen Jetta.'

'Right, sir,' Ahmed said, taking it.

'And there's something else. Did you find DS Crisp?'

'No sir. He's not in the station and he's not answering his mobile.'

Angel grunted and continued up the corridor. Then he suddenly stopped, turned round and went back down to the open CID room door.

'Well, find him, Ahmed. Haven't seen him all day. For all I know, he could have left the force and got a posh job running his own security business … counting Heather Mills's money … or pushing a pram for Madonna. *Find him*! Tell him I want to see him, pronto.'

'I'll see what I can do, sir.'

Angel reached his office and slammed the door. The phone rang. He reached out for it.

'There's a man, a Peter Meissen, in reception to see you, sir,' a young PC said.

'Right. Bring him down to my office.'

He replaced the phone and stared at the pile of post on his desk. He rubbed his chin. It never seemed to get any less. He sat down and began to finger through it.

The phone rang again. It was Ahmed.

'Have you found him?' Angel said.

'No, sir. That car registration number you just gave me … it's a double-decker bus in Dorset.'

'What?' he bawled. He sighed. 'Right, Ahmed. Inform Traffic to look out for a 2006 silver Volkswagen Jetta saloon with that registration number. The car was last seen in Bromersley town centre. The driver, male. Aged forty-five to fifty. Six foot two inches. Clean shaven. Dark hair. Well-spoken. Using the name George Fryer.'

'Right, sir.'

He banged down the receiver. His eyes narrowed as he thought about the elusive Mr Fryer. He could have kicked himself. He should have shown more patience. He may never find out the man's interest in the candle-snuffer. He'd known at first glance that he wasn't a newspaperman. His suit was too smart. His shoes too clean. He always thought that reporters got their clothes out of the dustbin: the same place most of them get their stories.

There was a knock on the door.

'Come in.'

It was the young police constable from reception, escorting a short, lumpy man in a Reid and Taylor worsted suit that didn't fit his awkward figure. He looked like an expensive gift, wrapped in a hurry. He hobbled in, every step required effort, and he smiled as though his underpants were too tight.

'Peter Meissen, sir.' The man held out a big hand on a short arm.

Angel shook it. It was as cold as a toad's belly.

'Please sit down,' Angel said, and he reached down to the bottom drawer in his desk and took out a brown paper bag with the word EVIDENCE printed in red across it and placed it on the desk top, but well away from his visitor.

'Now, may I see the item, Inspector?'

'Some identification, if you please, sir?'

Meissen nodded. 'I hope my passport will suffice?' he said and reached into his inside pocket.

Angel took it and noted that it was issued by Le Presidente, La Republic de Patina, Muerlin Strasse Officie, Westlenska, Balkan Etat de Patina. He also noted the passport number. Then he opened it. Looked closely at the photograph and the embossing to check that they had not been tampered with, noted Mr Meissen's address in Patina, then glanced through it at the visas. They seemed to consist only of the UK, France, Norway, Italy and the USA.

Angel handed back the passport with a nod and said, 'Thank you.'

'I hope you are satisfied,' Meissen said.

'That's fine, Mr Meissen. Where are you staying at present?'

'At the Feathers Hotel here in Bromersley.'

Angel nodded. 'Now what is your interest in the candle-snuffer?'

'I tell you, Inspector. Cards on the table. In Westlenska, in Patina, Inspector, I am a lawyer, and I have the honour of representing the Radowitz family, which in the 1930s was the most influential family in the city, both politically and commercially. They were also great supporters and benefactors of the church. However, in the thirties and forties, the years leading up to and including the Second World War, their possessions, their crops, land and farms were systematically plundered by the German occupation forces. As were millions of others. You will know of this? Also, some of the family were murdered. Now, more than fifty years later, the Radowitz family have recovered and prospered; they are now trying to reclaim the lost land, farms and valuables … whatever they can, wherever they can.'

Angel nodded. 'And you think the candle-snuffer may have belonged to the Radowitz family?'

Meissen smiled. His pants must have been shrinking even more.

Angel passed the EVIDENCE bag over to him. 'Even if it does belong to your clients, you know I can't release it.'

'To know positively would be one step nearer, eh, Inspector?' Meissen replied as he reached into the bag. He held the candle-snuffer up to the light and smiled, then he ran the finger tips of the other hand delicately over the engraved blades. It seemed to soothe him. He checked the scissor action, and then quietly, without looking up, said, 'And how did you come across it, Inspector?'

'A thief dropped it while running away from the scene.'

'And where was this?' he said, still looking down, smiling and caressing the piece.

'Can't tell you that, Mr Meissen.'

The smile left Meissen briefly but then returned. 'Did the thief take any other silver pieces?'

'I don't know,' Angel said, then added, 'Were there others?'

Meissen looked up and smiled again. His fingers moved up the blades of the snuffer to the silver hands at the tips. He slowly exercised the scissor action of the blades again.

Angel watched him. 'Is there some point in having the tips of the blades formed into hands?'

Meissen looked up at him brightly and said, 'When the scissors close, the hands come together as in prayer.' He closed the blades. 'So.'

Angel saw that it was so. He blinked. He hadn't realized it before. 'It is a religious piece?'

Meissen sighed deeply before he replied. 'It is from the Roman Catholic Cathedral of St Saviour's of Patina. It was stolen with twenty other valuable pieces, and it must be returned there as soon as possible.'

The phone rang. He reached out for it. 'Angel.'

It was Gawber. 'I'm in Johannson's hotel suite at the *Grand Imperial*, sir. SOCO have been and gone. The place is a tip. Looks like it has been turned over by somebody before they arrived. *They* wouldn't leave it like this.'

'Right. I'll speak to SOCO. Have a word with the manager, the chambermaid and room service. See if anybody saw anything. And get back here as soon as you can.' He rang off.

Angel wrinkled his nose. Nothing was ever straightforward. He wondered what Mark Johannson might have owned, that would be worth turning his room over for. Of course, thieves could always expect to find something they could sell.

He tapped out DS Taylor's number.

'Don, you've just done Johannson's pad in that Leeds hotel. Did it look as if it had been turned over before you got there?'

'Yes, sir. And very thoroughly too … it was a real mess.'

'Professional job?'

'No, shouldn't think so, sir.'

SEVEN

Gawber coughed, then coughed again. Angel stared at him across his desk, waiting for him to stop.

'Excuse me, sir,' he said. He turned away.

The coughing continued.

He took the little bottle out of his pocket, unscrewed the top and took a sip. He let it run to the back of his throat. The coughing stopped.

Angel watched him. He looked concerned. 'Why won't you go and see your doctor, Ron? Get you some proper jollop.'

'I'm all right, sir. My wife swears by this.' He took another sip, screwed the top back on and pocketed the bottle.

'I'm sure I can find a better use for that paint stripper or whatever it is.'

'It's all right, really.'

Angel sighed. 'You were telling me about Johannson's hotel bedroom.'

'Yes, sir. His hotel bedroom and sitting room were an absolute mess, sir. Everything had been turned out. We've brought all his clothes and stuff back in my car.'

'I'll want to go through it with you, sometime soon.'

'I spoke to the manager, the hall porter and the chambermaid, who was on room service some of the time. Nobody saw a stranger go into Johannson's room any time yesterday, but in the course of conversation the chambermaid told me that she had seen a young woman knocking on his door and being admitted on at least two occasions. She didn't see her leave … she had no idea if she stayed all night or not.'

Angel pulled a face like he was standing over the drains in Armley jail. 'A girl on the game?'

'Couldn't be sure, she said. Tidy black hair. Medium height. Classy black dress. Unusual tattoo of a spider on her right ankle. A tarantula.'

Angel sighed. 'A tarantula? Whatever next?' he said, then his eyes narrowed and he pointed a finger at him. 'We've got to find her, Ron. If she's been in his company these past few days, she could be very valuable to us. That's a job for Trevor Crisp.' His lips suddenly tightened. He looked up. 'Have you seen that lad anywhere?' he bawled.

'No, sir.'

'I don't know where the hell he gets to.'

'Here are the statements, sir,' Gawber said quietly, and placed a file he'd been holding on the desk. 'We spoke to everybody. Well, everybody on Sean Tattersall's list. Convivial lot, those film people. On the bottle, partying and eating all hours. All of them had alibis and had others to support them, all except one – the cameraman, Harry Lee.'

Angel's ears pricked up like a terrier hearing the opening of a packet of digestives. 'Hmm. What did he have to say for himself?'

'That he left the set at about five o'clock and drove his own car from the farm back to The Feathers. He had an early dinner on his own, went back to his room and didn't see anybody until breakfast this morning.'

'Hmm. Right. That simplifies things. There are only two of that lot that haven't got an alibi, and they are Otis Stroom and Harry Lee.'

Gawber raised his eyebrows. 'I know the murderer is likely to be a man, sir, but has Nanette Quadrette got a rock-solid alibi? She's noted to be a bit of a firecracker.'

'Looks like it. She was with her boyfriend all night – or that's what she *says*. And that's what *he* says.'

Gawber thought for a moment. 'That means you don't believe them?'

'I'll have to think about it,' he said wiping his hand across his mouth.

'Before all this, sir, I was trying to ID that dead tramp. Do you want me to get back to that?'

'No. Get Scrivens to sort that out. It'll be good practice for him. I want you to look into the background of Otis Stroom and Harry Lee. They're our priority now.'

There was a knock at the door.

'Come in,' he called.

It was a smiling Crisp who came bouncing in. He was a thirty-year-old handsome man in a suit as sharp as a newly stropped razor. He was popular with the girls, but not always popular with his superiors.

'Been looking for me, sir?' he said flashing a smile.

Angel's eyes glowed like searchlights on Strangeways tower. His cheeks went the colour of a judge's robe. He turned to Gawber and through tightened lips, said, 'Push off, Ron. I'll see you tomorrow.'

Gawber knew the score. He glanced at Crisp and then back at Angel as he closed the door.

Angel looked up at Crisp. He didn't know where to start.

'I know you've been trying to get in touch with me, sir,' Crisp began lamely.

'What's the matter with that bloody phone of yours?' Angel bawled.

'Nothing, sir.' The pupils of Crisp's eyes slid from left to right and back again. He knew he was in trouble.

'Well, why the hell was it switched off?'

Crisp reached into his pocket and took the mobile out. 'Was it? I don't know.' He looked at the LCD screen. 'Well, it's switched on now, sir.'

'If that phone isn't reliable, ditch it and get a new one,' he bawled. 'And tell Ahmed the new number so that we can keep in touch.'

'It works all right, sir. *Really*,' he added with as much earnestness as he could muster. 'I must have been in a bad reception area. Or it was the atmospherics.'

'Atmospherics!' Angel bawled. 'I'll give you bloody atmospherics. Yesterday, I sent you to find out about the occupant of Number 2, Creeford Road. Then you disappeared. Where did you go to, that's what I'd like to know?'

'Only making enquiries, sir. That's all. When you start from scratch it takes time. Now can I tell you what I found out?'

It was useless. Angel could not sustain antagonism with the lad at that level. 'It'd better be good,' he growled.

Crisp opened his notebook. 'Number 2, Creeford Road is occupied by a Richard Mace, aged fifty-seven. Born 6 April 1950. The town hall records show he's lived there a long time, over twenty years. Paid his community charge as regular as clockwork. The Inland Revenue say that on their books, he's down as divorced two years ago, one daughter, not now dependent on him. Doesn't pay any tax. He's not a cleric, according to Crockfords, and he's not registered with the medical council, so he isn't a medic. He's not a member of Whites, Annabels or Heneberrys; the others wouldn't tell me. His doctor said he hardly ever sees him. Not disabled or ill. Nothing unusual there. Has a full, clean driving licence. Running a new four by four Range Rover. That's about it, sir. Oh, I nearly forgot. There's nothing known about him on the PNC.'

Angel rubbed his chin. He had to allow, it was a pretty good result. 'What did he do before he retired?'

'I couldn't find that out, sir. The Inland Revenue said that their records on him didn't go that far back because for the last eight years he had not been in a tax paying bracket. They've got him down as "consultant," but they didn't know in what particular business.'

'Right. Now that's what makes it dead fishy. If he really was a consultant, in most any job, he'd have been earning a taxable income. And what's he living on now? What's consultant mean anyway? You could be a consultant anything.'

'Do you want me to stick with it, sir? Might be able to ferret it out.'

'No. I've got another job for you. More in your line. You know the Imperial Grand Hotel in Leeds?'

His face brightened. 'Yes, sir. Very posh place.'

'There's a girl. In her twenties. Tidy black hair. Medium height. Classy black dress. With a tattoo of a tarantula on her right ankle.'

Angel arrived at his desk at 8.28 a.m. as bright and shiny as the Chief Constable's MBE. He'd slept the sleep of the innocent and was ready for battle. He pulled his chair up to the desk to attend to the accumulation of letters and reports awaiting his attention. On top of the pile was a booklet with the words: 'Home Office Publication' on the cover. When he spotted it, his nose curled up. Part of the battle against crime was the requirement for him to read, mark, learn and inwardly digest this sort of printed porridge. He picked it up, noted it had sixty-four pages, and read the title: 'Revised rules and estimated costs for the cancellation of the recent proposal to amalgamate the police forces of North Yorkshire, West Yorkshire, South Yorkshire and Lincolnshire.'

He opened it up to pages two and three. Glanced at it, sniffed, then turned back to the front cover.

'Good. The answer, my dear Watson, is in the title,' he muttered then tossed the booklet into the waste-paper basket in the knee hole of his desk and returned to fingering the remaining letters and papers in the pile.

The phone rang. It was only 8.30 a.m. It was early. He reached out for it.

'Angel.'

From all the coughing and wheezing, he recognized the caller was Harker. His lungs made more animal noises than the boiler in Strangeways kitchen.

'Come down here,' Harker spluttered and banged down the phone.

Angel turned up his nose. He wondered what the Yeti wanted. He could hardly be expecting a result on the Johannson murder. The body was only found yesterday morning: he thought he had done pretty well. The other murder investigation into the tramp wasn't progressing quickly, admittedly, but he *was* on top of it. He was still awaiting SOCO's findings. And he had already applied for a search warrant for 2 Creeford Road following the funny business with Richard Mace, the householder and the girl thief dropping the candle-snuffer.

Angel knocked on the door and pushed it open.

There was more coughing from 'Mr Mean'. His face was buried in a handkerchief but he pointed to a chair and Angel sat down. A wave of TCP drifted past him.

'You wanted me, sir?'

'Yes,' Harker said with a sniff. 'I most certainly do.' He put the handkerchief away and picked up a sheet of A4 by the corner and waved it at him. 'What's this? What's this?' he said impatiently.

Angel peered at it. He thought he could see perfectly well what it was. It was his application for a warrant to search Number 2, Creeford Road.

'What's the matter with it, sir? I have set it up for later this morning.'

Harker shook his head. 'You can't do *that*! There's not enough justification.'

Angel's eyebrows shot up. 'The householder has no visible means of support, sir!'

'Have you any evidence that he's robbing banks or knocking over security vans or something?'

'That's what I want to find out, sir.'

'Have you some evidence that he's committed an offence?'

'No, sir.'

'Is he a past offender, then?'

'No. But there's the business of the girl coming over the wall with the stolen candle-snuffer.'

'You know it's stolen, do you? You've seen it on some missing list somewhere, have you?'

Angel's pulse was racing. 'Not exactly, sir.'

'Isn't Mace disowning it?'

'The girl dropped it, and when it was recovered and taken round to him, he said it was his, then changed his mind when my wife told him I was on the force.'

'Yes. I've read all that. I read all your reports. They're better than Hans Christian Anderson. Perhaps he made a mistake.'

'Perhaps he didn't?' Angel said angrily.

Harker glared at him. 'You can't keep poking into people's houses on some flimsy suspicion. We don't want a reputation for unnecessary aggressive policing. I know that you think that you have some special gift for solving difficult murder cases. And you have had some … small successes in the past, but you mustn't think that you are some superior body that can sniff out a criminal, like a talented water diviner can find a new underground source.'

Angel wondered if there was some praise in there somewhere. The Yeti must be slipping; he might say something complimentary if he wasn't careful.

'I don't think that at all, sir.'

'I should think not. Haven't you got plenty to do with those two murder cases? Shouldn't you be looking for the girl with the tattoo on her ankle?'

'Yes, I have plenty to do, sir. Plenty,' he said quietly.

'Right,' Harker said with a sickly smile. 'And so have I. You'd better get on with it.'

Angel could see that whatever he said, Harker had dug his heels in and was not going to sanction the warrant. It was frustrating that his efforts should be hindered in this way. He should be getting support not obstruction, but it had always been the same with King Kong.

He looked up and saw him screw up the application for the warrant and triumphantly throw it at the wicker waste-paper basket in the corner of the room.

Angel's blood pressure was up. He could hear his heart banging under his shirt. He went out and closed the door. That wasn't the end of the matter. Oh no. There was some mystery concealed inside Number 2, Creeford Road and he was determined to get inside the big house and find out what it was.

Angel opened the door, and the shop bell rang out.

Ahmed followed him inside, took off his helmet and stepped down into the little, low-ceilinged shop. He gazed round in surprise at the tightly packed mishmash of furniture, pictures, clobber and rubbish in Mr Schuster's little emporium.

David Schuster shuffled through the bead curtain in a cloud of cigarette smoke. When he saw Angel and Ahmed, he smiled, 'Ah. Inspector Angel, with reinforcements, I see, this time,' he said with a grin. 'What can I do for you?'

'This is Police Constable Ahaz,' he said turning round to Ahmed. 'Mr Schuster.'

They exchanged nods.

'I am glad you have called in, Inspector. I have remembered something about that candle-snuffer. The hands at the end of the blades. They are praying hands. It was something unique to a particular part of the low countries, many, many years ago. Of course the area was overrun by the Germans in 1939. Churches were looted. Church valuables were scattered all over.'

'I know that now,' Angel said.

Schuster looked surprised. 'Who told you that? There are not many people out of that part of Europe who would know about the praying hands, Inspector.'

'Who have you been telling about this candle-snuffer, Mr Schuster?'

'Nobody, Inspector. Nobody. Knowledge is money. I don't give information away lightly.'

Angel didn't believe him. 'I need to know,' he said commandingly.

'I didn't tell anybody,' Schuster said reaching for the burning cigarette he had placed there and taking a drag. 'That info didn't come from me. Must have been somebody else.'

'There isn't anybody else. *You* must have mentioned it to somebody.'

'I'm not daft, Inspector. I don't tell people my business. All my transactions are confidential. Knowledge and privacy are my stock in trade.'

Angel shook his head. This man could keep his mouth shut.

'I would have bought it from you at that price,' Schuster added with a smile.

'What price? It was never for sale. It still isn't.'

'Between £30 and £100, I said.'

'It's not mine to sell.'

'Now that we know where it came from, I could pay a £1000.'

'*It's not mine to sell!*' Angel shouted.

Schuster shrugged. '£2000?'

Angel shook his head impatiently. 'I said it's not mine to sell.' He sighed. 'But there is something I might buy from *you*.'

Schuster pursed his lips, affecting indifference and looked over his glasses. 'What is that then, Inspector?'

Angel looked down at the shop floor and gently tapped one of the fire extinguishers with the toe of his shoe. 'What do you want for this?'

Schuster blinked. 'A fire extinguisher? Can't sell you *that*. Health and Safety and all that. It would most likely be illegal. It probably doesn't work anyway. I've got six of them. They're over forty years old. Came out of Bransby Art Gallery.'

'What are you going to do with them?'

He shrugged. 'Probably end up on the tip.'

'Well, can I have one, then?' Angel said. 'For nothing. That wouldn't be illegal.'

'It probably doesn't work. Be all corroded up. It's no good, I tell you. What would you do with it?'

Angel tapped the side of his nose with his forefinger. 'Knowledge and privacy are my stock in trade. I don't give information away lightly.'

Schuster frowned then smiled.

EIGHT

There was a knock on Angel's door.

'Come in,' he called.

It was Ahmed: 'Just had a call back from the Salvation Army, sir.'

'Oh?' Angel said, looking up from the desk.

'They've no report of anybody missing who fits the description of our dead tramp.'

Angel growled and shook his head.

The phone rang.

'Make me a cup of tea. Two sugars.'

Ahmed headed for the door, frowned then turned back. 'You don't take sugar, sir.'

'I do today,' he grunted as he reached out for the phone. 'Angel. Hello, yes?'

It was DI Matthew Elliott of the Antiques and Fine Art squad based in London – an old friend of his. Angel's face brightened.

'Got your message, Michael,' Elliott said. 'I've studied the photograph of the candle-snuffer. Great stuff. How did you come by it?'

'Not so fast,' Angel said, rubbing his chin. 'What's your interest in it?'

'What do you mean? It comes under the heading of Antiques and Fine Art. Of course I've an interest in it.'

'Is it stolen?'

'Of course it's stolen.'

'Who is the rightful owner?'

'I suppose the Orthodox Cathedral of St Saviour's of Patina, the West Balkans.'

Angel blinked. 'What's it doing in Bromersley then? It's not that valuable, is it?'

'Not in itself, no, but you'd be surprised.'

'Surprise me, then.'

'Well, it's a long story, Michael. I've looked it up in old cabinet papers in the war archives.'

'Just give me the gist of it.'

'Well, I have been able to discover that back in the dark days of the Second World War, when Europe was being invaded and overrun by Germany, and the land was being pillaged and treasures stolen for Goering and other high ranking Nazis, the priests and elders of the orthodox church in Patina decided to send the cathedral silver and treasures via England to a bank in New York, for safe-keeping. So the old silver communion sets and pictures and things, twenty-one pieces altogether, were carefully packed in two wooden crates and smuggled out of Yugoslavia, through France and across the Channel. It was an involved and complicated operation. Special permits and custom exemption forms had to be completed, and the two-man RASC squad, transporting them from Harwich to Liverpool needed a special government movement order and fuel allowance, and had to have petrol vouchers issued by the Ministry of War. The consignment had to be delivered to Liverpool docks, Pier 16, SS *Bellamy*, bound for New York, on 15 December 1940. It was addressed to account number 9045, East Balkan Bank, Manhattan, N.Y. This was all done at a very high level and Prime Minister Churchill approved the arrangement. However, tragically, the SS *Bellamy* was sunk by a U-boat in the mid-Atlantic on 17 December and it was naturally assumed that the treasure had gone down with it. A detailed report was written up at the time in the cabinet secretary's office and a copy sent to the cathedral in Patina. This report was first made public in 1971. Since that time, in fact, until two days ago, it was thought that everything had been lost until your photograph of that candle-snuffer, that very particular candle-snuffer, was shown to the church authorities. It became clear that the consignment *wasn't* at the bottom of the Atlantic.

'Now, I have been very hard at it since. The last known sighting, which I have been able to trace, is of the two-man squad transporting the treasure through Sheffield, on 14 December 1940, which was the first night of the terrible blitz they suffered there. Just before midnight, a Police Constable Thomas Shaw, who incidentally must have been a very brave man, recorded in his notebook that he gave the officer in charge directions out of Sheffield, to Bromersley, then over the Pennines to Liverpool. He also recorded that they were travelling in a 15-cwt Morris van, licence plate number RA 1767, and that the officer was a man called Captain Mecca or similar. They couldn't quite read his writing.'

'Mecca? Was he foreign?'

'Don't know. There the trail ends.'

Angel shook his head and rubbed the lobe of his ear between finger and thumb. 'Are we to assume then, that wherever the candle-snuffer came from, this collection of church silver and treasures will be there also?'

'I think so, hopefully. Don't you?'

'And what sort of value are these … treasures?'

'Priceless, Michael. Absolutely priceless. The candle-snuffer was one of the least valuable of the items. Don't bother trying to put a figure on them. Whatever you or I thought, the next appraisal would probably double it, and the one after that might very well multiply it by ten. It's just a big, big … telephone number.'

'That much?'

Elliott said, 'You didn't tell me how you came by it.'

'No. A thief dropped it as she was climbing over the wall of a house.'

'A man?'

'A girl.'

'You've searched the house?'

'No.'

'*What*?' he screamed.

Angel's lips tightened back against his teeth. He knew that Elliott would think him incredibly stupid.

'Why not, for god's sake?'

Angel sniffed. 'I have a little ... local difficulty,' he said.

The phone rang.

He reached out for it. 'Angel.'

It was DS Crisp on the line. He sounded in trouble. He was talking fast and breathlessly. 'I'm in the gents at the Imperial Grand, sir. I've found her.'

Angel's head lifted, his eyes front and centre. He didn't believe it. 'The girl with the tattoo?'

'Yes. She's a countess. Contessa Radowitz. The thing is ... I am trying to hold on to her with a drink at the bar.'

Angel sighed. 'Well, don't leave her, son,' he snapped. 'Get back to her before she evaporates with the booze!'

'Yes, sir. I will. I know, but I have no money. Well, not this sort of money anyway. I've only twenty pounds. A round of drinks here costs twelve quid!'

Angel's face dropped. 'Daylight robbery.' He bit his lip. 'I'll sort something out. Stay with her. Keep working on her. Find out what you can about Johannson. Phone me at your next opportunity.'

'Right, sir. Got to go.' The line went dead.

Angel replaced the phone and reached into his back pocket. He pulled out a roll of notes. He counted out ten £20 notes and put the roll back. He pushed the £200 in an envelope and put it into his inside pocket.

He went down the corridor past the cells and out of the back door. He got in his car and drove to Leeds. He was there in forty minutes. He parked on a meter up Edward Street and walked back the hundred yards to the Imperial Grand Hotel. He went past the reception and porter's desk, and followed the signs to the bar. It was a big room and busy with lots of noisy people sitting and standing around. He went up to the bar and ordered a fresh orange juice. He had to wait until it was prepared, which suited him fine. It gave him the opportunity to check out the room. There was no sign of Crisp, with or without a girl. He wrinkled his nose.

The bar girl placed the orange in a long stemmed glass on a paper doyly in front of him. He paid with a note, she came back with his change. He counted it, pulled a face like an undertaker at a pauper's funeral, dropped the coins in his pocket and carried the glass out through the door into the foyer. He saw an illuminated sign that said 'Toilets' and another 'Lounge' and meandered into the latter. It was another big room with many easy chairs and settees set around coffee tables. There were about thirty people in there … mostly in pairs. Then he saw Crisp and the young lady, sitting on a settee, talking. There were coffee cups and a cafetière on the table in front of them. Even from that distance Angel thought the girl looked good. Jet black hair. Small, slim. He drifted back into the foyer. By the lift he found space on a tall wooden pedestal with a big vase of flowers on it to rest his glass, then he stood with his back to the wall, fished out his mobile and tapped in a number. It was soon answered.

'I'm here in the hotel in the foyer,' Angel said quietly. 'I've brought you £200's worth of bait. Can you meet me in the gents loo?'

'Certainly,' Crisp said flamboyantly. 'I can agree to that. Buy me £30,000's worth. Debit my Swiss account with it. It can be partly set off as a tax loss against the gain I made on the sale of my yacht in Italy. Be in touch soon.' The line went dead.

Angel smiled and shook his head. The stuff that lad could make up at short notice. He'd jailed conmen who weren't half as smooth as Trevor Crisp.

Angel finished the orange, put the glass down on a table as he passed it and made his way down the steps to the gents loo. He checked all twelve cubicle doors to find out if they were occupied. Two were but they were shortly vacated. He ran the taps over the sink and hovered over the washbowl in case anybody came in. A few minutes later Crisp came through the door wearing a worried look.

'Thank you for coming over yourself, sir,' he said hurriedly. 'You should have sent somebody.'

Angel frowned. 'Have you found out about Johannson? What she was doing in his room?'

'Haven't got round to that, yet. Can't ask her that outright, sir, and maintain my cover,' Crisp said.

Angel nodded. 'Well, I must see her and ask her directly. There's something else. You said her name was the Contessa Radowitz?'

'That's right, sir. Flavia is her Christian name.'

'Radowitz is the family name of the owners, I think, of the candle-snuffer. I had their family lawyer to see me, trying to get possession of it.'

Crisp glanced at his watch. 'I ought to get back to her, sir. We don't want her disappearing.'

'I'll go up to her. I'll ask her directly about Johannson. I won't mention you. Give me ten minutes or so.'

'Yes, right,' Crisp said.

'Before I forget. Get me her fingerprints. She might be on file. You never know.'

'Right, sir. You brought me some money, sir?'

'Oh yes.' He handed him the envelope. 'Don't throw it around. It's honest people's money, that is.'

A man came through the swing door.

'Have a nice day,' Angel quipped and caught the door on the swing. He ran up the steps and made for the 'Lounge'.

He was glad to find the young woman still where he had first seen her. She was holding a coffee cup in her hand. He weaved his way through the furniture until he was standing directly in front of her.

She was in a plain black dress. She wore a silver cross on a silver chain round her neck.

He looked down at her. He checked the ankle for the tattoo of the spider. It was there and showed conspicuously through glossy black stockings.

'Excuse me,' he said. 'Are you the Contessa Flavia Radowitz?'

She looked up, her mouth dropped open. Then she smiled. It was the sort that melted icebergs. He liked looking at her.

'You catch me at a disadvantage,' she said replacing the cup in the saucer.

He opened his wallet and took out a business card. 'Detective Inspector Angel of Bromersley Police. Might I have a word with you, ma'am?'

'Of course,' she said with arched eyebrows. She gestured for him to sit next to her.

'Thank you.'

'I cannot imagine what you might think I have been up to, Inspector.'

'I'll come straight to the point … ma'am.'

'Flavia is fine,' she said. 'Everybody calls me Flavia.' Her English was excellent, but there was a pedantic carefulness in her diction that showed it was not her mother tongue.

Angel nodded. 'Flavia, I am investigating the death of Mark Johannson, the film director,' he said.

She looked straight into his eyes. She wasn't happy. 'Yes, I knew him,' she said evenly.

He was surprised at the coolness of her reply. 'He was staying in this hotel. I understand that you visited him in his suite here from time to time.'

'Yes. Twice, actually.'

'What were the reasons for your visits, might I ask … Flavia?'

'Oh,' she said, seeming relieved. 'Not very wicked reasons, Inspector. We met at the bar here by accident the day he arrived.'

'What day was that?'

'Saturday. Did I say by accident? Coincidence would be the more correct word. He made some comments, flattering comments about me … about my appearance. He told me he was a film director, that he liked what he saw, and suggested that he might be able to get me a leading role in a film he was directing. He said that the actress currently in the role was difficult and may leave or get the push.'

'Really?'

'He suggested that we had dinner together in his room … to discuss the possibility.'

'And what was your reaction?'

'Naturally, I was flattered … even excited at the prospect. The first evening was spent discussing his work as a director, the character I might play, how much I could earn and so on. It was very illuminating, interesting … very exciting. We had a few drinks and then I left at about eleven o'clock. The second evening, however, was very different. It seemed that to seal the deal, he required me to spend the night with him, in his bed.'

Angel wrinkled his nose and looked at her.

'I didn't want to do that,' she said unemotionally. 'He wasn't a nice man, Inspector.'

'So you left?'

She nodded. 'And I never saw him again. When I heard on the radio that he had been murdered, of course, I was surprised … but … that was all.'

Angel understood her perfectly, but he was not pleased. It didn't progress his investigation one bit.

'Thank you very much,' he said. 'In your conversation with him, did he happen to mention which part in which film he was considering you might be suitable for?'

'Yes. The character was Cora, the girl who meets and marries the lead, Otis Stroom, and the film was a biography of some great Englishman, Edgar Poole. I don't know of him. Is he well known hereabouts?'

Angel noted that such a move, if it had been seriously contemplated, would certainly have put Nanette Quadrette's nose out of joint. He wondered how she would have reacted if she had known about this proposition.

'Oh yes. He was a famous artist. You could not be expected to know our local history. Might I ask what part of the world you are from?'

She lowered her eyes briefly. 'It used to be known as Yugoslavia.'

'And what brings you to Yorkshire?'

She hesitated. 'Just a holiday, Inspector.'

Angel looked at her and rubbed his earlobe. He wondered whether to press her for the truth. There were about a million other places in the world that would have been more fun than Leeds in February.

There was a knock at the door.

'Come in.'

It was DS Don Taylor. 'Got a minute, sir?'

'Of course.' He always had a minute for the forensic lads; they were often the source of information that led to a conviction. He would find as many minutes as necessary.

'What is it, Don? What you got?'

Taylor carefully placed a plastic credit card in front of him. 'Found that stitched into the lining of the coat being worn by the tramp, sir.'

Angel frowned, picked it up, stared at it, then looked up at Taylor and said, 'And is it his?'

'I don't know, sir. His prints were on it. Nobody else's. It's been through a cash machine a few times, by the look of it. It's still valid. More than a year to run.'

Angel peered at the embossed name. He read it aloud. 'Alexander Bernedetti.' He looked up at Taylor. 'Ring any bells?'

'No.'

Angel thought he had heard it somewhere, but he couldn't think where. 'Right. I'll take it from here.'

Taylor smiled. 'Thought you would.'

'Great stuff, Don,' Angel said. 'I'll want to see the stitching, the coat, how it was actually concealed.'

'Anytime, sir.' He went out and closed the door.

Angel rubbed his chin. This was progress. Progress indeed. He reached out for the phone and tapped in a number. It wasn't immediately answered. He checked his watch. It said 2.12. He waited. And waited. He depressed the telephone cradle and then tapped the redial button, and waited, but it still wasn't answered. He banged down the handpiece and peered closely at the credit card. It was with the Northern Bank, and its expiry date was 3/08. He turned it over. It was signed in the strip on the back: 'Alexander Bernedetti'. It looked all right. Of course, you can't tell how good a credit card is simply by looking at it. He checked his watch again. It said 2.13. He blew out a yard of breath. He stood up, pushing the chair back with his knees, dashed out of the room and down the corridor to the CID office. The door was open. He looked in. There were four detectives busy at their desks by the windows, but there was no sign of Ahmed.

'Anybody seen PC Ahaz?'

'No sir. No sir.'

Angel nodded. 'When you see him, tell him I want him straight away, will you?' he said crisply.

'Yes sir. Right, sir.'

He returned to his own office and slowly closed the door. He sat down at the desk and rubbed his chin. It wasn't like Ahmed to be inaccessible. That was more the style of Trevor Crisp who was always missing and impossible to contact for one reason or another.

Angel picked up the phone again and dialled Ahmed's mobile number. It was soon answered. He got the standard recorded message explaining the phone was switched off. Angel slammed the handset back into the cradle and rubbed his chin a few times rapidly.

NINE

Two hours later, Angel had substantially reduced the thickness of the paperwork on his desk. Some had gone in the waste-paper basket, some had been filed, and some had been read, ticked and relaunched on a set journey round the station for the edification of others.

There had been more important things he should have been doing, but under the unusual circumstances of the afternoon, he didn't want to be away from the office when Ahmed Ahaz eventually made his appearance.

The church bell pealed out the Westminster chime. It was four o'clock. It would soon be pitch black outside.

The phone rang.

The civilian receptionist said a Mrs Ahaz was on the phone to speak to him. Angel nodded and sighed. He was relieved and pleased. She was no doubt phoning to explain her son's absence.

'Good afternoon, Mrs Ahaz. And how are you?' he said cordially.

'Ah, Inspector Angel,' she began. Her voice was shaky and speaking an octave higher than normal.

Angel frowned. He knew something was wrong.

'Is my son Ahmed there … with you?'

'No, Mrs Ahaz. I have not seen him since lunchtime. I thought that you were going to tell me why he had not returned to work this afternoon.'

There was a pause. He listened attentively. He could hear her breathing unevenly.

'Something has happened to him,' she said in a small voice. 'I'm certain of it. He was to have met me under the clock in Meadowhall at a quarter to one. We were going to choose a new suit for him. But he never turned up. At first I had thought something had cropped up and that you had kept him over his lunch break. I waited and waited. Then I came home. I expected a message from him. Oh dear, Inspector, what am I to do?'

Angel rubbed his chin. Ahmed was a totally reliable young man. Something unusual must have happened. His first thought was the hospital in case Ahmed had been knocked down in traffic, or some sudden illness had overtaken him.

'Is there anywhere he might have gone, Mrs Ahaz?' he said. 'Has he any friends or relations he might suddenly have decided to visit?'

'No, Inspector. No. If he had, he would have told me. He would have phoned. He wouldn't have had me standing under a clock for an hour waiting for him.'

Angel knew that was so. He couldn't imagine where the lad might be.

'I'll immediately start making enquiries, Mrs Ahaz. He won't have got far. Don't worry. Are you speaking from home?'

'Yes.'

'Are you on your own?'

'Yes.'

'I'll send a WPC to keep you company.'

'There's no need to.'

'When your son turns up, she can report it to me. Save you the trouble. Now, stay there, by the phone. He might turn up or ring in any minute. And try not to worry.'

He replaced the phone and dashed out of his office, up the corridor to the end and turned left to the uniformed inspector's office. He knocked on the door and pushed it open. There was nobody there. He spat out a four letter word. It sounded like 'well', but was dry as a bone and as hot as a crematorium. He came out and closed the door. Then from behind, he heard the regular marching of polished boots on a composition floor. Coming down the corridor strutted Haydn Asquith, buttons gleaming, and wearing a smart new flat hat with a big black peak that almost touched his nose. He was the uniformed inspector at Bromersley.

'Haydn,' Angel said. 'Just the man.'

Asquith came up to him and stopped. 'Looking for be, Michael?' he said loudly. He was seriously in need of attention to his adenoids.

'I need your help, Haydn. I've got a lad missing. Over three hours now. PC Ahmed Ahaz.'

Asquith raised his head. 'Yes? I dow him. Nice lad. What can I do?'

'My team are all out. Can you let me have a WPC to liaise with his mother?'

'Yes. Leisha Baverstock. It'll be overtime for her in an hour.'

Angel nodded. 'Ta.'

'Anything else?'

'I need somebody to do the hospitals.'

'The patrol cars can do that. I'll tell them to report back direct to you. I'll sort it straight away,' he said and opened his office door.

'Thank you,' Angel called.

'He'll turn up. You'll see,' Asquith said, then he gave a quick smile and closed his door.

An hour later, it was cold, black and foggy outside on the streets of Bromersley.

In Angel's office, he watched a fly land on the lampshade of the light on his desk. It walked slowly up it, then round the top, then stopped on the brim. It rubbed its back legs together, then just stayed there … impertinently, boldly, defiantly. It just stayed there.

Angel thought that if he could slyly pick up the big brown envelope, which contained the annual report of the PIA (Police Inspectors' Association) that was on the pile in front of him, he could give that fly a mighty belt and finish it off, once and for all. His hand moved slowly over the desk. With the absolute minimum of movement, he managed to get a grip on the envelope, slowly lifted it, aimed and was about to belt it one, when it flew away. It went in a zigzag route up to the ceiling then over the steel cupboard out of sight.

Angel tossed the envelope aside and returned to staring at the paint on the wall. He had been staring at it for too long.

He heard the church clock chime five. He checked his watch. He had been in the office a good hour; nobody had knocked at the door; nobody had tried to contact him on the phone; he had heard nothing along the corridor outside; everywhere was in absolute silence.

It was as quiet as a druggie shooting a twist of Class A into a main artery.

He could have phoned Mrs Ahaz, but that might have stopped Ahmed from getting through to her. He could have phoned his wife, but that would have blocked his phone from incoming calls.

He was running short on patience. He wouldn't be able to do nothing for much longer.

He didn't have to.

The phone rang.

'Ah,' he gasped and snatched it up. 'Angel.'

'PC Donohue, sir. I've been patched through. Inspector Asquith said I should speak to you direct.'

'Yes. Yes,' Angel said quickly. 'You've news of Ahmed Ahaz?'

'No, sir. I've just done the General Hospital on Sheffield Road and I've also done Skiptonthorpe Hospital. No young man answering his description has been admitted today.'

Angel silently groaned. His chest began to burn up. 'Right, lad. Ta.'

'Can I do anything else, sir?'

'No. No. I don't think so,' he said rubbing his chin. There was a throbbing in his ears.

'I'll keep my eyes peeled, sir. There's probably a very simple explanation.'

'Probably,' Angel replied but in his heart of hearts, he didn't really think that there could be. He began to fear the worst. He bit his lower lip as he slowly replaced the phone.

He looked at his watch. It was 5.04. He reached back out for the phone and tapped in a number.

Gawber answered.

'I wanted to catch you before you leave,' Angel said. 'Ahmed's missing. Been missing since lunchtime. He's not at home. His mother's phoned in. I can't pretend I'm not worried.'

There was a moment's silence, then Gawber said, 'I'll come straight down, sir.' And he did.

Angel told him all that had happened.

Gawber nodded but could offer no suggestion that Angel hadn't already considered.

'I can't sit around much longer,' Angel said. 'I'd be better touring the streets on the off-chance that I might see him.'

'It's dark out there, sir. You wouldn't see anything.'

'Could stop and ask people if they've seen him.'

Gawber shook his head. Angel knew he was right.

Suddenly there was a knock at the door.

Angel turned, pulse racing, dashed across to it and pulled it open. It was big John Weightman, a burly uniformed constable of the old school.

'What is it, John?'

The prompt opening of the door took Weightman by surprise. 'There's a funny carry-on at reception, sir. There's a man … found outside … sort of tied up … asking for you.'

'Tied up? What? It's not Ahmed Ahaz?'

'Oh no, sir,' Weightman said. 'No. An unusual little man … looks like he's been knocked about a bit. He says he knows you. Wants to see you, urgently.'

Angel and Gawber exchanged glances.

'Right,' Angel said and they followed Weightman out of the office, up the corridor through the security door into the reception area.

A young PC came out of the interview room by the reception room door. 'I've put him in here, sir. Sat him down. I almost fell over him ... he was in the gutter opposite the front door. Tied up. I've taken the plaster off his mouth and eyes and untied the rope round his wrists and arms.'

'Right, lad. Let's have a look at him.' He bustled his way past the young constable into the small interview room followed by Gawber to see a rumpled figure of a man seated at the table. He was screwing up his face and rubbing his wrists.

'Ah! Inspector Angel,' the man cried out and leaped to his feet as soon as he saw him.

Angel's eyebrows shot up as he instantly recognized the man. It was David Schuster. He was in his dusty, dishevelled suit, shirt and tie. His face was troubled, red and perspiring, and his hair was tousled. On the table was a coil of rope and two adhesive plasters, the kind used to dress injuries.

Angel went up to him. 'Mr Schuster. Are you all right?'

'Inspector Angel. They've got your young police constable, and I'm afraid they mean business.'

Angel felt as if he'd been hit in the chest by a cannonball. He swallowed. At the same time he put out his hands to Schuster's arms and returned him to the chair. 'It's all right. Sit down. Who have? Tell me about it.'

Schuster reached into his top pocket and pushed a folded printed letter into his hand. 'They sent me with that. It's a ransom demand for the lad.'

Angel took it and read it.

To DI Angel,

Your young copper will be returned alive in exchange for the Patina treasure. Put all the 21 pieces in a white bin bag and tie it up securely with string, not sticky tape. Place on the pavement on blue chalk mark in shape of a cross at kerbside at crossroads at bridge arches on Wath Road, Bromersley at exactly 5.55 pm this evening then go away quickly. On safe receiving of all 21 pieces of treasure, your copper will be released. No tricks or he's dead.

Angel's face looked as if he was himself staring death in the eye. He handed the letter to Gawber and walked away, his hand massaging his chin.

Gawber read it and said, 'We don't have the stuff, anyway, do we?'

'Well, we don't know for certain *where* it is,' Angel said. 'And we certainly can't get it and drop it as instructed at the arches on Wath Road in forty-five minutes.' Angel turned and leaned over Schuster. 'Who are these people?' he asked.

'I don't know. Four of them came into my shop this afternoon. Demanding to see the candle-snuffer. They thought I had it. They scared me, I can tell you. Huge men in dark overcoats. Do you think they're the mafia?'

'Could you detect an accent?'

'I don't know. They might have been Londoners.'

'No idea who they might be?' Angel said.

'No,' Schuster replied.

'Were there any more than the four you saw?'

'I only saw four. I don't know.'

'Did you see PC Ahaz?'

'No.'

'Have you any idea where he is being held?'

'No.'

'Did they talk about any … place at all?'

'No.'

'Well, tell me quickly exactly what happened. Don't miss anything out.'

'Well, I was in my shop as usual. At about one o'clock, I suppose it was, four big men came in and asked to see the candle-snuffer from the Patina Collection. I told them I didn't have it and explained that you had shown it to me. They were angry. At first, they didn't believe me. Then they found some rope in the shop and fastened me at the wrists then my arms, then coiled the rope around me. They put plasters over my eyes and my mouth, took me outside, put me in a car and covered me with a blanket or something like that. I was in that car, worrying, for some time. I believe that while I was in there, they searched my shop. Then the four piled into the car with me and drove off. They stuffed that letter in my pocket and told me we were going to the police station and that they would be turning me out there, that I was to find you urgently and deliver the letter to you personally. Next thing, the car stopped, they pushed me out onto the pavement and drove off. I had no idea where I was. I couldn't see. I tripped up over something and fell down in the gutter. Then somebody came up to me. One of your policemen. He peeled off the plasters, untied my hands and asked me who I was and what was I doing. I told him. I then realized where I was. He brought me in here. And that's all I know.'

Angel brushed his hand through his hair and strode about the room. 'There'll be some little thing they said, or hinted at, that might give us a lead as to where they took Police Constable Ahaz,' Angel said staring at him.

Schuster looked blank. 'Can't think of anything.'

'There's got to be *some*thing. Did you hear anything? Any unusual sound? Apart from the words they spoke?'

'No.'

'Did you notice any particular smell while you were with them? Garlic, mints, snuff, anything?'

'No.'

Angel sighed, looked at his watch, turned to Gawber and said, 'We've only got thirty-six minutes.' Then he jabbed a thumb in Schuster's direction instructing Gawber to have a go at questioning him.

Angel walked round the room rubbing his chin.

At first, Gawber looked blank. He couldn't think what to ask. He turned to Schuster and said, 'Are you sure you didn't detect any hint of where they might have taken the lad?'

Schuster shook his head forlornly.

Angel said, 'How many of the four men spoke to you?'

'Only one.'

'And did you notice his accent, or any mannerism, tattoo, rings? Did he smoke? Did he have a moustache, beard, spectacles. Did he wear a hat? How was he dressed?'

'He was smartly dressed. Suit, collar and tie. And he might have had a London accent, I told you that. No mannerisms, tattoos or jewellery. I didn't see him smoke. He hadn't any facial hair or specs.'

Angel suddenly brushed his hand through his hair again. He swivelled round to Gawber and said, 'This is getting us nowhere.'

Schuster shook his head. He looked down at the floor and said, 'I'm sorry. I'm no help. I'm not used to this.'

He looked like a frightened rabbit.

'That's all right,' Angel said as gently as he could manage. 'Let's go back to your shop, to where this started. Something might occur to you. We might be able to pick up a lead from there. It's our only chance. We'll go in my car. Come on. Hurry up.' He turned to PC Weightman on his way out, he pointed a finger at him and said, 'I look to you John to contain this situation. I don't want it spreading about. The media mustn't get hold of it or it may cause the abductors to panic. Tell nobody, and instruct those here who know about this, if they care anything about Ahmed's safety not even to talk about it among themselves. All right?'

'Right, sir.'

Angel, Gawber and Schuster piled into the car.

TEN

It was a cold, dark, mean night. There was a heavy frost and wisps of fog sailed past in the headlights as they made the rapid three minute journey to Schuster's antique shop.

Angel stopped the car in front of the big old mill. The businesses on the ground floor had closed leaving the old building in ugly winter darkness.

Schuster led the way. Angel and Gawber followed, shining powerful police issue torches on him as he unlocked the shop door. Inside felt colder than outside and smelled of stale cauliflower water and unwashed socks.

Schuster fumbled along the wall for the switch, and turned on the lights.

Inside was an absolute shambles. Pictures, antler's heads, furniture and curtains were piled up everywhere. It seemed that every item in that cramped up little shop had been examined and cast aside: the mess was indescribable.

Angel took one look and said, 'If there was anything of value here they would have found it.'

Then he suddenly had a strange feeling in his stomach. He knew something was wrong. Very wrong. He whipped round to Schuster and with staring eyes, through clenched teeth, said, 'The shop door was locked. I thought you said you were in the car, tied up, with sticking plaster over your mouth and eyes under a blanket when the shop was being searched.'

Schuster's eyes bounced. 'I was. I was. Yes, that's right,' he said, licking his lips.

Angel grabbed the little man by the collar of his suit and lifted him up by it. He glared into his eyes and said, 'And I suppose when they'd finished ransacking this place and not finding what they were looking for, they put out the light, locked the shop door and carefully put the key back into your trouser pocket?'

'No,' he stammered. 'No. I don't know what they did with *that* key. I opened the door with the *spare* key.'

Angel didn't believe him. 'Oh? You always carry a spare key with you, do you?' Angel said tartly.

'Yes.'

'You always carry the regular key *and* the spare key, do you?' he added even more heavily.

'Yes.'

'In the same suit?'

There was a moment's hesitation. 'Yes.'

'And when we got here just now, you didn't even try the door to see if it was open. You didn't need to. You knew it was locked, because *you locked it*.'

'No. I didn't lock it. I guessed it would be locked. Or I supposed it would be, or it was just habit. I don't know.'

'You're a liar, Schuster. There's something else that's just come to me. Only hours after showing the candle-snuffer to you, I had enquiries from two very peculiar individuals. I know the informant must have been you, because only you, my wife, DS Gawber here and myself knew of the candle-snuffer's existence. Everybody else thought it and the rest of the church treasure was at the bottom of the Atlantic.'

'It's not true,' he protested.

Angel knew that it wasn't exactly true. The resident of Number 2, Creeford Road knew, but Schuster wouldn't have known that.

'You and a crooked mate of yours have got my lad, Ahaz, haven't you?'

'No,' Schuster yelled indignantly. 'I don't know what you're talking about. I swear it.'

Gawber stood there with his mouth open.

Angel turned to him and said, 'Have you got any cuffs?'

'No, sir,' Gawber said.

'It's not true,' Schuster persisted. 'I don't know anything about your colleague, Ahaz. What I have told you is absolutely true, every word.'

Angel glanced round the shop. He saw a sticky tape dispensing machine on the counter. The tape was about half an inch wide. He leaned over, dragged it across, turned it round and pulled out about a yard of it.

'What you doing?' Schuster said, his shining eyes flashing round in all directions.

Gawber hesitated. He looked very unhappy at what Angel was about to do.

Angel yelled, 'Hold your wrists out, together.'

Schuster protested, 'No. I've done nothing wrong. No. You can't do this to me.'

Angel's mouth tightened. He glared at Gawber urging him to assist.

Gawber reluctantly pulled the man's forearms out in front together, while Angel wrapped the sticky tape roughly round Schuster's slim wrists, drawing them tight together.

Schuster struggled, but the two policemen were too powerful for him, and when they had finished the tape seemed to be as restricting as purpose-made handcuffs would have been.

'I protest,' Schuster yelled. 'I'm totally innocent. You can't do this to me!' He wriggled vigorously to check out the effectiveness of the tape, and let out an uncontrolled scream of anger when he discovered that it seemed to be 100 per cent efficient.

'I'll have a look round,' Angel said, his face scarlet and his heart thumping. He jumped over the glass counter and landed noisily on something wooden that gave way and splintered.

'Go easy,' Schuster said. 'It's my stock you're damaging. I expect to sell that commode to somebody one day.'

Angel extricated his foot from the debris, made his way round the back of the counter, through the bead curtain to a tiny place with a desk and chair and more junk beyond to a door. He pushed it open to show a lavatory and wash basin. It was unoccupied. On the whitewashed wall was a coil of rope looped around a bracket. He snatched it down and dragged it behind him. He turned back towards the bead curtain and stood there in the centre of the room a moment, thoughtfully.

Then he called out, 'Ahmed. Are you there? Ahmed!'

He listened. There was no reply. He sighed and made his way back through the debris to the customer side of the counter.

Schuster noticed the rope he was carrying. 'Here. That's my clothes line. What are you doing with it?'

Without a word, Angel dropped the coil of rope over Schuster's head. It settled round his neck and waist like he was a mountaineer.

Schuster struggled. He was unable to discard it. 'What's happening? What are you doing?' he protested irritably.

Angel touched Gawber on the shoulder. 'There's nothing back there,' he said. 'Come on. He must be somewhere in this building. There are five floors to search. We've no time to lose.'

'There's nothing in there,' Schuster said, anxiously.

Angel dashed out of the shop into the night, his breath showing white in the street light. He dragged the reluctant Schuster to the graffiti-covered main doors to the upper floors of the mill. They looked as if they hadn't been opened for years. He turned to Gawber and said, 'Get those doors open. There's a battering ram in my car.'

'I tell you, there's nothing in there,' Schuster said firmly.

Gawber looked at Angel. 'Crack on with it, Ron. There isn't a moment to lose.'

Gawber turned away to Angel's car. Two minutes later, the door was damaged enough to make entry possible.

'Nobody's been in there for fifteen years, to my knowledge,' Schuster protested. 'It's not safe. The stairs could give way at any time.'

'Just tell us where Ahmed is,' Angel said patiently.

'I don't know,' Schuster shrieked. 'I don't know. I keep telling you, but you don't listen. *I don't know where he is*! I don't know anything about anything. You've got me all wrong! *Honestly*!'

Angel and Gawber flashed their torches around the entrance way. There were steps downwards as well as upwards.

'Let's take the cellar first,' Angel said, and flashed the torch down the stone steps and along white flaky walls. They made their way down to dusty stone floors. It was icy cold and every sound echoed round the cobweb-covered walls. He led the way followed closely by Schuster and Gawber.

They reached the flagged basement floor and Angel called out, 'Ahmed! Ahmed! Are you there?'

They listened for a few moments. There was no reply.

Schuster said, 'You're wasting your time. He's not here.'

Angel and Gawber flashed the torches around. They could see the length of the long empty floor area interrupted only by thick pillars of stone. At the far end of the area, Angel saw what looked like a door. He ran down the full length of the building to it. He could then see that it was a door made in iron and had a huge lock and handle on it with a large key sticking out. He pulled quickly at the handle. The door was very heavy. He managed to open it and look inside. He flashed the torch around. All that was inside the little room was a stone table, nothing else.

'What was this used for?' Gawber asked. 'Built like Fort Knox. It looks like the place you might store explosives or valuables.'

'It was for storing expensive dye stuffs and dangerous chemicals for curing and preserving lamb skins,' Schuster said, superciliously. 'I told you he wasn't in there.'

Angel turned back on him. 'Where is he then?' he said wildly. 'What have you done with him?'

'I don't know anything,' Schuster whined.

'Come on!' Angel shouted as he ran back to the steps. They climbed to the ground floor, passed the main door, and flashed the torch around at the long empty floor space, which was interrupted only by metal support pillars. Some of the street lights shone through the dirty windows onto the ceiling.

Angel's heart thumped heavily as he climbed the steps. Time was defeating him and there was no certainty that Ahmed was even in the building.

'I'll take Schuster straight up to the top floor, Ron. Check off the rest of the building and follow us up there.'

'Right, sir,' Gawber said. He was not a bit happy with the situation. He had no idea where Ahmed could be and he didn't think that his boss seriously thought that he was concealed in the building either. It was just something to be doing … somewhere to be looking … a long shot if ever there was one.

Angel pushed the nervous Schuster in front of him up the stone steps. At the top of each flight, Angel stopped and yelled out, 'Ahmed, are you there? Are you there, Ahmed?'

He stopped and listened.

When they reached the fifth and top floor, and after Angel had called out to Ahmed once more, Schuster said, 'He's not here. It wouldn't be safe to bring a dog in here.'

'Where is he then?' Angel bawled angrily, his face red, his chest burning. 'Where is he?' he screamed. 'What have you done with him?'

Schuster shook his head. 'I haven't done anything with him,' he stammered. 'I'm just … the messenger. You know what they say, don't shoot the messenger. I don't know any more than you do.'

Angel growled and shook his head. He went over to two big doors in the outside wall that faced the head of the steps. He shone the torch on them to see if they could be opened. He found a hasp and unhooked it. There was a handle. He applied pressure to it. The door was on runners. It squeaked and moved a little. He applied more weight. It suddenly gave way and slid open about eight feet. A blast of icy air hit him in the face.

They could hear the distant hum of traffic down below.

'What you doing?' Schuster squealed, looking down into the cold, evil night at the lights coming and going through the drifting fog. 'It's dangerous. You want to keep that door shut, it's dangerous.'

Holding tight onto a handrail strategically placed by the sliding doors, Angel then leaned out into the night and pulled into the building the metal arm with a pulley wheel attached, which was on a swivel on the outside wall.

Schuster knew something was amiss. His eyes flitted rapidly in every direction. 'What are you doing? What's happening? I have rights. You can't do this to me. I shouldn't even be tied up like this. I am not an animal.'

'Sit down … on the deck,' Angel ordered as he lifted the coil of rope Schuster had been carrying.

'What for? What are you doing now?' he said, eyeing him distrustfully.

Angel came round the back of him and tapped the back of his knee with the side of his shoe. 'Sit down,' he snapped.

Schuster went down and landed clumsily on the floor. 'Hey! What are you going to do?'

Angel quickly took one end of the rope and looped it round the man's ankles.

'What's happening, Inspector?' he chattered, waving his shackled hands about and casting a glance out of the open door. 'What are you doing? You can't do this to me. I'm a tax-paying citizen. I've never done a dishonest thing in my life. I shall report you to the chief constable. I'll have you drummed out of the force.'

Angel ignored the bleating. He tied the knot round his ankles very tight and pulled against it to check it.

'What you doing? Trussing me up like this. What for? What's happening? Stop this. Stop this at once. I am an innocent man.'

Angel fed the other end of the rope through the pulley and pulled it tight. The first two yanks took up the slack, the third began to drag the horizontal, handcuffed man along the floorboards towards the open doors.

Schuster's breathing was as noisy as a steam train. 'What you doing, Angel?' he squealed. 'What you doing? You can't do this to me. It's an infringement of my civil liberties. It's not legal. It's inhuman! I've told you everything I know. You can't do this!'

A flash of a torch preceded Gawber's arrival on the top step. He saw the trussed up Schuster sliding towards the open door, and Angel yanking the rope round the pulley wheel.

'What's happening?' Gawber yelled desperately. 'What are you doing?' He dashed over to where Angel stood. He looked down the side of the building to the road below.

'Don't get too near that door, Ron,' Angel said.

'You can't do that, sir!' Gawber screamed.

Angel didn't reply.

Schuster shrieked. 'No! No!'

'This pulley and stuff's all old. It's not safe,' Gawber said putting a hand on his arm.

Angel's eyes glowed like a madman. He pushed Gawber away.

Schuster shrieked. 'I don't know anything. I've told him all I know. Stop him, Gawber. He's gone raving mad! Let me go!'

Gawber said, 'You can't do this, sir. He can't tell us anything more.'

Schuster was only inches from the open door, his ankles already hanging outside over the edge, and the rope to the pulley wheel was taut.

'Move out of the way, Gawber,' Angel bawled. 'Or you might get knocked down when he swings out.'

'No! No!' Schuster screamed.

He looked down at Schuster and said, 'For the last time, where is my constable and what is the name of your accomplices?'

'I don't know,' Schuster cried. 'I've told you, I don't know, because I don't.'

Angel raised his arms to yank the rope.

Gawber said, 'You can't do this. It might not carry his weight. You might kill him. Stop it!'

Angel gave the rope a mighty yank.

Schuster's legs slid across the floorboards and went up in the air followed by the rest of him.

He swung upside down over the road below in the cold night, screaming like a banshee on hot coals. He swung to and fro four times like a pendulum. He screamed louder at each swing, then suddenly out of the blackness, he yelled, 'All right, Inspector. I'll tell you all I know. Pull me in. For god's sake, pull me in.'

The rope steadied then began a slow rotating action.

'Stop it moving and pull me in. Have some pity, for god's sake.'

Angel hung anxiously onto his end of the rope and said, 'Talk, Schuster. Talk.'

'It's my landlord. I owe him four month's rent. If I don't pay him, I'll be out in the street. He promised me £100,000 out of this deal. I was going to retire. That's all I know. Now pull me in.'

'And what's your landlord's name?'

He didn't answer straight away. Then he said, 'He'll kill me for telling you. It's Jondorf. Harry Jondorf. Now pull me in, I beg of you.'

'And where's my lad, Ahmed?'

'I don't know.'

Angel released his grip momentarily. The pulley wheel turned a quarter of a revolution. Schuster dropped twelve inches and stopped with a jerk. The machinery rattled dangerously.

He screamed. '*Don't do that. I honestly don't know*!'

'I could so easily let go of this rope and you'd go sailing down into the street below.'

Schuster groaned. 'I don't know where your man is. Honestly, Inspector Angel. He said he didn't trust me with all the details. Jondorf said he would deal with all that side of the job himself.'

Angel continued. 'Who else is in this … crooked scheme of yours?'

'Nobody else. Just the two of us.'

'Thought so. And where do you think Jondorf has got my lad stashed away? You must have an inkling.'

'I don't know.'

'Well, where do you think?' he bawled.

'I've really no idea. I've told you all I know. For pity's sake, pull me in.'

Angel's mobile phone rang. He was going to ignore it. He looked across at Gawber, who said, 'Might be about Ahmed.'

Schuster groaned, 'Pull me in, Inspector. I've told you all I know.'

With one hand Angel gripped the rope while he fished in his pocket for the mobile. He pulled it out and passed it across to Gawber, who opened it, listened for half a minute or so, muttered something into it, then switched it off and passed it back to him.

'It's from a uniformed patrolman, Evans, sir … about a saloon car with false number plates you wanted a report on. Well, it has just been seen with a driver fitting the description you gave of the man calling himself George Fryer, speeding up Wakefield Road. Evans has lost him, but he thought you'd want to know.'

Angel's eyebrows shot up. He looked through the dark at the man on the end of the rope. 'That's one of the two people who approached me, Schuster, that I referred to.'

Schuster said, 'It's the same man. That's the other name he uses.'

'What do you mean?'

'Jondorf and Fryer are one and the same. He bought this mill from a man called George Fryer. He uses the name for some business things. Now for god's sake pull me in. I'm feeling sick. I'm going to throw up. I'm going to die.'

Angel's brain was working faster than a Broadband connection. 'Where is he now?'

'He'll be at the railway arches ready for the pick up, I suppose,' Schuster wailed.

'But why was he speeding on Wakefield Road? It's nowhere near there.'

'Dunno. He owns some property up there, and he garages his own cars there. He has several. Now please pull me in.'

Angel brightened. 'Lock-ups?' he said. 'Whereabouts?'

'Don't know. Somewhere on the Watersley Estate.'

'How many?'

'Don't know. Please pull me in. I'm feeling dizzy.'

'What's the time, Ron?' Angel asked as he reached over to the pulley wheel arm, swung it in, and quickly slackened off the rope to lower Schuster to a horizontal position on the deck.

Schuster gave a huge sigh and made no effort to move or sit upright.

Gawber shone his torch on his wrist. '5.35.'

'We'll never make it,' he said. He turned to Schuster. 'Somebody will come back for you. Don't go anywhere.'

Schuster groaned: he knew he couldn't move.

The two men made for the stairs.

ELEVEN

It took Angel eight minutes to reach the Watersley Estate off Wakefield Road. Most houses had lights in their windows. Householders were obviously snuggled up for the evening. He quickly toured round it and his heart sunk. He found lock-up garages all right, but there were such a lot of them. Watersley Estate was extensive and he supposed there must be one lock-up for each household or flat.

The estate consisted of four huge blocks of flats. Next to each block was a row of lock-ups. There were eighteen in a row, opposite another eighteen, then near the next block of flats another eighteen, times two, then again, twice more. That totalled a 144 lock-up garages.

Angel returned to the first block and stopped his car. He stared at Gawber and said, 'Where are we going to start?'

Gawber shook his head. It seemed an impossible task. 'We can't break into *every* lock-up. There isn't time. We don't even know if Ahmed's hidden in *any* of them. Or even if he's still alive.'

Angel wrinkled his nose, shrugged and said, pointedly, 'What else can we do? Where else should we look?'

Gawber nodded in agreement and they both leaped out of the car.

'You take this first block and I'll take the block opposite.'

Angel went up to the first lock-up garage and banged the torch three times on the metal door, then shouted, 'Ahmed! Ahmed! Are you in there?' Then he waited, ear to the door, listening for the slightest noise, while silently counting to ten. 'Are you in there, Ahmed?' When he heard nothing, he moved to the next lock-up and repeated the exercise. Meanwhile, Gawber went through a similar routine along the row opposite. They each finished a block of eighteen in about five minutes and met at Angel's car. If it had been daylight, each would have seen the look of despair and hopelessness on the other's face.

There was nobody about. They were lone voices in the night. It was too cold for civilized people to be outside. The cold was getting colder, the fog thicker, the night blacker and the quiet unnerving. It was the sort of night a dowdy little woman somewhere might be feeling the edge of a carving knife while eyeing the fat neck of her drunken husband.

Angel and Gawber got in the car to move onto the second block.

Gawber said, 'Do you think our time would be better spent chasing after this Jondorf character? If we could arrest him, he might then tell us where Ahmed was.'

Angel sighed. 'I don't know. It's full of ifs and mights, isn't it? He'd not be inclined to tell us where Ahmed was, because by that he would be admitting his guilt. So it isn't as easy as all that. The physical well-being of Ahmed is, without doubt, our first priority. Once we have found him and done the best – the very best – we can for him, then we can put our best efforts into finding and arresting Jondorf.'

Gawber nodded. He had to agree. His boss always had the knack of analysing a situation and making sound decisions.

They started the knocking and calling business on the next two blocks of thirty-six garages. Time was not on their side. Then, at the next to the last garage, of his eighteen, Angel thought he had a response. He banged the torch three times on the metal door, then shouted, 'Ahmed! Ahmed! Are you in there?' Then he waited, ear to the door, and listened and thought he heard a faint banging noise. Two, three, four, then five times.

His heart leapt.

He called again. 'Ahmed! Ahmed! Is that you?'

He held his breath, listened and heard the same banging noise. His pulse raced.

'Hang on in there, Ahmed. Hang on. We're coming in for you! Won't be long!'

Gawber heard Angel's whoops and ran across. 'How are we going to get in, sir?'

They eyed the door, and the lock on the handle, and tried to turn it. Of course, it was locked.

'Brute force,' Angel said. 'There are two tyre levers in my boot.'

Five minutes later, they had the door off its hinges and leaning against the next garage. They shone their torches onto a car. It was the one with the false number plates that sailed out of the car park of the Fat Duck. Angel's pulse throbbed in his ears. There was more banging from the boot. Angel opened it up. He shone a light on a slim figure in police uniform, hands and ankles tied with rope and with tape over his mouth. It *was* Ahmed. He blinked in response to the torchlight. Angel's heart pounded as he removed the tape with a quick pull.

'Are you all right, Ahmed?'

'Yes, sir. I am now,' he said brightly. 'Am I *glad* to see you, sir?' he said with a big smile.

Angel felt a warm glow in his breast. But he sniffed and said, 'I'm docking you a half day's pay for being absent without permission.'

Ahmed grinned.

'It should be a lot more,' Angel added. 'Where's Jondorf?'

'Who, sir?'

'The man who kidnapped you.'

'Don't know, sir. He dumped me here a while ago.'

Gawber pulled out a scout knife and began cutting through the rope.

'How did you let yourself get into this mess?'

'He had a gun, sir. I didn't have much choice.'

Angel's eyebrows shot up. He exchanged glances with Gawber. 'A gun? What make of gun?'

'A handgun, sir. Don't know what … make … or model.'

'Did you see his face? Would you be able to recognize him if you saw him again?'

'Oh yes,' Ahmed said smiling confidently.

That sent a shudder down Angel's spine. Ahmed didn't realize it, but Jondorf must have intended murdering him. If Jondorf had intended no harm, he would certainly have taken precautions not to be able to be identified by him.

Angel and Gawber helped Ahmed out of the car boot. He seemed all right. All were much relieved. They made for Angel's car.

'What time is it, Ron?' he said as they climbed into the car.

'It's 5.50, sir.'

Angel started the car and pointed the bonnet towards the main road. 'Phone HQ and ask them to get a driver to call in the armoury and draw out a Walther PPK/S and a full clip of eight rounds, in my name. I know it's a bit unusual, but tell him it's an emergency. Then tell him to meet us asap, no blues or twos, at Low Lane on the way to Wath Road arches. I want him to take Ahmed home.'

'Right, sir,' Gawber said pulling out his mobile.

Angel turned out of the estate onto the main road and headed down towards the railway arches.

Gawber busied himself on the phone and the arrangements were soon completed.

Then Angel said, 'Ahmed. Have you got your mobile?'

'No, sir. The man took it off me.'

'Borrow the sergeant's and phone your mother and be quick about it. Tell her you're all right, you'll be home in a few minutes, and she can kill the fatted calf.'

Ahmed blinked and looked puzzled at Gawber as he took his phone. Gawber merely smiled.

Ahmed made the call. There was rejoicing and a few tears at both ends of the phone. Angel swallowed and smiled thankfully.

'Ahmed,' Angel said. 'Before you leave us, I want your shirt. Get it off.'

The young lad stared at Gawber looking for an explanation. Gawber shrugged.

'And has anybody got any string?'

Nobody had any string.

'And your tie,' Angel added.

Ahmed looked amazed, but he knew better than to question it.

A few minutes later as they ran onto Low Lane, only a minute from the railway arches, Angel stopped the car and took Ahmed's shirt and tie round to the back of the car and opened the boot.

A police car glided silently behind him and stopped. The driver got out.

'There's your taxi, Ahmed,' Angel yelled. 'Give my best wishes to your mother.'

'Thank you, sir. Yes I will.' Ahmed transferred quickly to the police car holding up his jacket collar. He was without a shirt and tie and the night was getting colder. The driver settled Ahmed in the car and came up to Angel busy with something in the car boot.

'Good evening, sir.'

Angel turned to the uniformed patrolman. He thought he recognized him. 'PC Donohue. You got a firearm for me, lad?'

'Sorry, sir. The superintendent wouldn't let me sign for it. He said you had to sign for it personally, or you could ring the FSU and request an Armed Response Vehicle.'

Angel dropped what he was doing. He flung both arms into the air. His eyes stuck out, his face went scarlet.

'I know all about that!' he yelled. 'I have an emergency situation on my hands! An armed man to deal with. There simply isn't time for all that crap.'

The patrolman's jaw dropped. He didn't know what to say.

Angel quickly recovered. He knew it wasn't Donohue's fault. He reached out to his arm and gave it a friendly squeeze. 'I'm sorry, lad. But I have a dangerous situation on my hands. An armed man. The last thing I wanted to do was face him unarmed.'

Donohue's face tightened. He totally understood the inspector. 'Can I do anything, sir?' he said earnestly.

'No,' he said slowly, rubbing his hand across his mouth. He pointed to the high-profile white, red and blue police car and said, 'That jam sandwich would give everything away. No thanks.'

'I'm sure I could do *something*, sir,' he said eagerly.

'No. It's important to take PC Ahaz home, asap. He's had a rough time. He needs a bit of TLC and his mother will be worried until she sees him.'

'If you are sure?'

Angel sighed and nodded. 'Aye.'

Donohue turned away.

Angel called him back. 'There is one thing, Constable.'

'Yes, sir?'

'Give DS Gawber loan of your cuffs tonight, lad. I know it'll make you improperly dressed, but I'll make it right with Inspector Asquith, if necessary.'

'No problem, sir. I'm going back to the station, anyway. I can pick up another pair from the stores.'

'Right. Push off then, lad. I'm working against the clock here.'

'All right, sir,' Donohue said. Then he saluted and said, 'Be careful.'

The patrolman unclipped his handcuffs from his belt and handed them through the open car window to DS

Gawber. They exchanged pleasantries, then Donohue made for his car.

'Good luck, sir, and good night,' he called to Angel as he opened his car door.

'Thanks, Constable. Goodnight.'

The car quickly pulled away into the black fog.

Angel soon finished cobbling together a package of wheel-changing tools, police manuals and a leather police holster into Ahmed's shirt and tied it all up with the tie. He looked at his handiwork, sniffed, closed the boot and brought the bundle into the body of the car.

'That's the best I can do,' he said, handing it to Gawber. He then climbed inside the car and drove off. They soon arrived at the arches.

'Ron, we've got to find a blue chalk mark. The note said it would be at the kerbside at the crossroads at bridge arches, Wath Road. I'll drive around slowly. Look out for it.'

'There it is, sir,' Gawber yelled. It was on the pavement, in front of one of the big arches, a heavily blue chalked asterisk that nobody could miss.

Angel stopped the car. Gawber opened the door and without getting out, simply lowered the shirt and contents onto the centre of the mark. Angel glanced around to see if he could see anything or anybody. Two cars passed in opposite directions but there seemed nothing out of the ordinary.

'Right, sir,' Gawber said.

Angel let in the clutch. 'What's the time?'

'5.55 exactly, sir.'

'Phew!' As he drove away, small pieces of sandstone unexpectedly splattered down on the car bonnet making quite a clatter. He leaned forward and peered skywards through the windscreen.

'What's that? Where's it come from?' Gawber said.

'Must have come from up there,' Angel said pointing a finger in the air. He drove ahead to get away from the scene, as instructed in the letter, then suddenly, after a minute or so, he stopped the car and blurted out excitedly, 'I've got it.

I've got it. He'll be up there on the viaduct, on the railway track, at this very moment, lowering some sort of a line with a hook on it, to lift the spoils. That's why he specified a white bin bag – so that he could spot it from right up there, at night – and to be tied with string, *not* sticky tape, to make it easier to stab a hook into it.' He smirked. 'I hope he'll manage to lift it by Ahmed's tie.'

Gawber blinked as he realized that Angel had worked out Jondorf's plan.

Angel went on excitedly. 'And he wanted the spoils placing there at 5.55 and not six o'clock, or a quarter past, because he intends to complete his escape by hitching a ride aboard the five-fifty train from Bromersley which will pass through there any time now on its way to Wakefield. We must try and stop him.'

'A cunning plan sir,' Gawber said. 'Worked out in every detail.'

'He has an evil mind,' Angel sighed as he looked at his watch. 'We are too late. The train will have left Bromersley now. And we can't possibly beat it to Wakefield, nor can we be certain he got on it.'

'Hmm. There must be something we can do, sir.'

'There isn't time, Ron. There isn't time. And I've been thinking. What will Jondorf do when he finds the spoils are not exactly what he expected?'

'He'll be one unhappy bunny, sir,' Gawber replied.

Angel sighed heavily. 'He'll want revenge.'

Gawber nodded. 'Yes. And he's got a gun.'

The night was now blacker than an undertaker's cat in a sack of soot, and billowing clouds of fog crowded round Angel's car headlights. The dashboard thermometer reading showed the outside temperature to be minus 4 degrees, and the car heater was on maximum.

'I've been thinking, Ron,' Angel said, as he teetered round the corner into the Watersley Estate. 'If Jondorf completed the journey on the train to Wakefield and had planted a car there in preparation, he could be back here … depending how bad the fog is on the motorway … in about five or ten minutes.'

Gawber nodded slowly.

'We'll have to move fast.'

They passed the hazy illuminated windows of the second block of flats and parked the car well out of sight, switched off the lights, locked it and walked back to the lock-up garage where Ahmed had been imprisoned.

'We've just enough time to set up a surprise party.'

'But he's got a gun, sir.'

'We have the advantage of surprise, Ron. He won't be expecting us; he won't know how many there are of us. He won't yet know that we have found Ahmed and released him.'

Gawber rubbed his chin.

'Let's have a quick shufti round his lock-up,' Angel said.

They flashed their torches in the small garage. At the side of the car was a discarded kitchen chest of drawers. There were a few tools and old car parts on top of it. Angel selected four small spanners and a six-inch long piece of copper petrol pipe on the bench, which he stuffed into his overcoat pockets. He saw two tyres hanging on a bracket in the wall. 'Here, we can use these,' he said enthusiastically. 'Help me down with them.'

Gawber looked bewildered.

'Put one at each end of the block.'

Gawber shook his head. He was thinking that they would not be much defence against a gun.

Angel knew what Gawber was thinking. 'Now let's put the door back against the front of the garage. Make it look as it was. We don't want him to suss the situation before we are ready for him. Let it look normal, as if we've no idea that he has Ahmed hidden in here. He'll likely come the same way we came because it's the nearest.'

Angel set out his stall the best way he knew how. He discussed tactics with Gawber and they took up positions together at the far end of the block. They switched off their torches and listened. They didn't have to wait long.

They heard the engine of a car. It was not possible to work out from which direction it was coming until its fog-shrouded headlights gradually appeared. It was heading for lock-up garage number seventy-one. It stopped, its headlights shining on it. The driver doused the lights, got out of the car and began to walk towards the garage door.

Angel stuck his head round the corner of the end of the garage block and said, 'Harry Jondorf, this is the police. You're under arrest. Put your hands up.'

There was a short silence, then a red hot pellet of lead shot past Angel's ear into the blackness.

Angel sucked in a lungful of fog. He hadn't expected such an immediate and aggressive response.

On cue, Gawber immediately raced on tiptoe along the backside of the lock-ups to the opposite end.

'You're not taking me in, Angel,' Jondorf yelled.

'You're under arrest, Jondorf. Put your hands up. If you hit any of my men with your random firing, I will charge you with a full list of firearm charges as well as abduction.' Then he called out, 'Sergeant Peters?'

From the other end of the block, Gawber called, 'Yes, sir?'

There was a second shot let off by Jondorf in Gawber's direction.

'I've warned you about that, sir,' Angel called.

Gawber then picked up the tyre and set it rolling off towards the next block of lock-ups, then ran in the opposite direction behind the next block, carefully avoiding being in silhouette from the light shining from the windows of the flats.

Jondorf didn't hear the tyre rolling, but he did hear it land on its side a few yards away from him. Then Angel set his tyre rolling along the concrete away from the block. It made just enough noise to be disconcerting to a man in almost total darkness. It stopped and fell the other side of him.

Two red shots of lead left Jondorf's gun aimed at the tyre.

'Constable Hemingway?' Angel called.

'Yes, sir?' Gawber called from behind the first block of lock-up garages about twenty yards from Jondorf.

Two shots rang out in that direction.

Angel smiled. They were really getting to him.

'Mr Jondorf. I must warn you that if you even scratch one of my men, with this wild gunplay, you will be charged with attempted murder.'

As he spoke, Angel threw a spanner towards the other block of lock-ups. It landed on some grass behind Jondorf on the other side.

'It is nothing less than reckless to be firing in the dark at my men like this.'

Another shot rang out.

Angel said, 'Don't be stupid, man. You're not going to escape. You're surrounded.' Then more loudly he said, 'Right, close in men. Use your nightsights prudently. Shoot only when you have Jondorf in vision. Aim for the legs. Not the vital areas.' Then he swiftly threw two more spanners in different directions in quick succession.

Suddenly Jondorf screamed, 'Don't shoot!'

'Throw down your gun,' Angel ordered.

Another piece of flying lead came in Angel's direction. It passed close by and made Angel very cautious. He reckoned that that was eight rounds spent. That was the usual number of bullets in a handgun. He didn't know whether there were any more to go. He baited him once more.

'That was very stupid, Jondorf.'

Angel heard the click of a firing pin of a gun with an empty magazine. And he heard it again. He knew Gawber would have heard it too.

Jondorf gasped.

Angel blew a short sigh of relief and yelled, 'Close in, men. Fire low at will.'

He heard Jondorf suck in air. He judged he was about twenty feet away.

'No,' Jondorf yelled.

Gawber called, 'I have him in my sights, sir.'

'Shoot him, then!'

'No,' Jondorf screamed. 'No. I give in. I give in.'

'Hold your fire, Sergeant,' Angel bawled. 'Jondorf, throw your gun towards me. Lie down on your stomach.'

'Get down. Get down. Get down,' Gawber bawled while running towards him from behind.

'Don't shoot!' Jondorf cried. 'Don't shoot!'

The discarded gun clattered on the concrete a few yards in front of Angel. He came out from behind the end of the block. He couldn't see anything. He pulled out the piece of petrol pipe from his pocket and held it like a handgun and then switched on the torch.

Spreadeagled on the floor in front of him was the wriggling body of Jondorf. He looked up, blinked, shielded his eyes from the glare and screamed, 'Don't shoot! Don't shoot! I am unarmed now. You wouldn't shoot at an unarmed man, would you?'

Angel pointed the petrol pipe at him and said, 'Right. Put your hands behind your back.'

Gawber came up behind him, pulling a pair of handcuffs out of his pocket.

'Harry Jondorf aka George Fryer you're under arrest for the abduction of Police Constable Ahmed Ahaz. You do not have to say anything ...'

TWELVE

'Good morning, sir. You wanted to see me?' Angel said.

'Aye,' Harker growled, then stuck his little finger in his ear, twisted it like a screwdriver, pulled it out, looked at it, blinked and said, 'Aye. Come in and sit down.'

Angel chose the chair nearest the door.

'I understand there was a bit of a flap on last night?'

Angel shook his head slightly. 'Not a flap, sir. It was a bit sticky at first, but it all came out right in the end.'

'I should have been informed. When one of my men is abducted, I should know about it.'

Angel couldn't think of an answer that would have shut him up, so he said nothing. He would like to have said that the super might have known something was seriously amiss when he had asked to be issued with a firearm via PC Donohue, which he had blocked, but he didn't think it was worth the effort.

'Is Ahaz all right?'

'Yes, sir. He's back at his desk this morning. Seems fine.'

'And what about the two accused?'

'Harry Jondorf aka George Fryer is in a cell, sir. I've already spoken to the CPS. They're satisfied that we have plenty to have him remanded, and subsequently convicted, so he should be off to Armley straight from court this morning.'

'Ah,' Harker said, appreciatively. 'And the other? The oily little antique dealer?'

Angel wrinkled his nose. 'He got away, sir. We left him tied up. We couldn't take him with us. He would have slowed us down. When we returned for him, he wasn't there. He must have worked his way free. I don't know where he is at the moment. I took a look at his shop early this morning. There's no sign of him there.'

'I'm surprised at you,' he sneered. 'Allowing a crook like that to slip through your fingers. Put out a bulletin. Get him picked up smartly.'

'I've already done that, sir.'

'Hmmm. I should think so,' he said then he picked up a small pink piece of paper out of a wire basket on the desk in front of him. 'And what's this?' he said with a sniff.

Angel glanced at it; he knew exactly what it was. 'Requisition for a new shirt and tie for Ahaz?'

He had anticipated argument about it. It was always the case when the claim was out of the ordinary.

The phone rang. Angel reckoned he was saved by the bell … for the moment.

The superintendent reached out for it. 'Harker … What's that, sir? … Where? … The gas board? Good heavens! … I'll see to it, sir … Yes, sir. Right away, sir.' He slammed down the phone and jumped to his feet. He stared at Angel.

'The chief constable. There's a UXB been found by gasmen working in the road at the junction of Doncaster Road and Creeford Road. The man that found it said it looked like a big one. We'll have to evacuate the area and close it off. I'll phone the army; it'll take them an hour or so to get here from York. In the meantime, find Asquith and get him to liaise with the gas board and block off Doncaster Road, Creeford Road and Shortman Street. I'll get my secretary to get the vicar of St Edward's to open the parish hall and have his ladies organize hot drinks and so on. Then get a squad together and begin to evacuate the houses and the pub on the corner quickly. If it's a tricky one, the residents may have to stay the night. Social services would need to be informed. All right?'

'Yes, sir,' Angel said, concealing a wry smile.

There were eight traffic wardens, twenty-two policemen and women in yellow dayglo jackets, swarming round both ends of Creeford Road, Doncaster Road and Shortman Street, which included Shortman Square. They were setting up diversion signs to block off roads around the junction to all vehicles except specified categories of emergency vehicles. One such vehicle was an unmarked police car driven by Angel. With him were DS Gawber, DC Scrivens and PC Ahaz. He drove the car purposefully the length of Creeford Road to the big house on the corner, Number 2. The residence was only ten yards away from the trench on the pavement from where the gasmen had reported finding the unexploded bomb in their diggings. There were no workmen in sight; an empty canvas shelter and eight traffic cones surrounded the hole; a shovel lay there dropped on top of a mound of fresh yellow earth.

Angel passed the roadworks scarcely giving them a glance and pointed the bonnet of the car through the open iron gates and round to the front of Number 2, Creeford Road. The four men dashed out, climbed the steps and ran up to the big door. Angel hammered the heavy black door with the knocker several times. They waited. Nothing happened. He repeated the hammering. Still nothing happened. He nodded to Scrivens who lifted up the battering ram he had been carrying and applied it to the door. At the third attempt, the door jamb splintered and the door sprang open.

Angel led the way and they rushed through a small entrance hall to an internal glass door comprising a richly engraved panel surrounded by a carved wooden frame. He pushed that open to discover he was in a commanding entrance hall. He stood and looked, amazed at what he saw. The three others gazed round in silence, utterly overwhelmed.

It was like going into the palace of the king of the world. Six larger-than-life stone carved statues of men and women were positioned around the side of the room against the walls, while the walls themselves were covered with huge, colourful paintings of men in knee breeches and women in wide skirts, groups of small families, naked fat women lounging on sofas, landscapes, seascapes, Mother and Child depictions as well as many other religious scenes. The two large high windows in stained coloured glass, showing grand scenes from the Bible, illuminated the grandiose scene in vivid reds and mauves. Underfoot were thick rugs of Persian design. The sight was majestic. The four men stood there in awe of the place. None of them had ever seen anything like it.

They wandered through an open door into more of the same, but with a table at the top of three steps, arranged like an altar with silver candlesticks, a jewelled paten and chalice, and behind, a triptych of jewelled collages depicting scenes of the Lord Jesus and his mother Mary, Jesus and the disciples fishing, and The Last Supper. The collages were created from gold leaf, rubies, pearls, diamonds and emeralds.

It was like the grandest cathedral ever seen.

Angel stood there so engrossed in the colours, the splendour, the richness and the beauty that, in his imagination, he could hear loud organ music accompanied by a hundred-piece orchestra with a predominance of harps and violins playing something very, very stirring.

The illusion was short-lived. He was brought down to earth by the sound of the door knocker coming from the front of the house. He dashed back into the main hall, down the passage through to the front door and pulled it open.

There stood an army officer in a flak jacket and khaki hat. He had 'Army Disposal Unit' flashes at the top of his sleeves and three pips on each side of his shoulders. 'Excuse me,' he said. 'Are you DI Angel?'

'Yes.'

'I saw the car. Your superintendent said you would be around here somewhere. Captain Morrell, Bomb Disposal Unit. Good news. You can halt the evacuation, Inspector.'

Angel's looked at him and nodded. 'Oh?'

'Rather a hoot, really,' he said with a grin. 'Just to let you know that the suspect bomb isn't a bomb at all. It's a false alarm. It's just an old fire extinguisher.'

'Really?' Angel said.

'Come in, Ahmed. Close the door.'

'Yes, sir?'

'I want you to get me the number of War Office Records. I want to speak to somebody in the RASC.'

'What's that, sir?'

'Run Away Somebody's Coming,' he bawled irritably.

Ahmed smiled. He knew he was being teased.

Angel shook his head. 'It stands for Royal Army Service Corps,' he explained patiently. 'It's time you knew all these initials. They are the part of the army that does its delivering and storing. I want to speak to somebody who keeps their personnel records. Then I want to speak to DI Elliott. He's with the Fine Art and Antiques squad in London.'

'Right, sir.' Ahmed stood up, turned and reached out for the door knob.

'There's something else,' Angel said. 'I think that Richard Mace must be planning to leave 2 Creeford Road very soon. It's probably getting too hot for him. Find out if he owns the place. If he does, he'll want to sell it. Find out which estate agent or solicitor is acting for him. Pretend you're an ordinary member of the public, you've heard a rumour that it's coming up for sale, and you're interested in buying it. We might find a lead to where he is now.'

Ahmed smiled. He quite looked forward to pretending to be somebody he wasn't. 'Right, sir,' he said and turned to go.

'I haven't finished,' Angel said, pulling something out of his pocket. 'I also want you to find out about this credit card. It's with the Northern Bank. It was found sewn into the coat of that tramp character found dead under the arches on Wath Road. It's in the name of Alexander Bernedetti. Here.' He passed it over the desk. 'See what you can find out about the man. You should get his personal details as well as his financial standing.'

'Right, sir.'

Ahmed went out as Crisp came in. He was carrying an envelope. When Angel saw him, he leaned back in the chair. His mouth tightened. He wasn't pleased.

'I didn't expect you back here,' he growled. 'You're supposed to be shadowing the beautiful Flavia.'

'Run out of money, sir.'

'Run out of money?' he bawled. 'You had two hundred pounds!'

'Doesn't go far with a bird like that, sir. She's impossible to impress. Anyway, I'm reporting back because, well … because she's gone, sir.'

'Gone? You … you just let her slip through your fingers? I expected you to stick to her as close as that tattoo.'

'She was there when I left her last night. This morning, she had booked out.'

'Where did she go?'

'Don't know.'

Angel sniffed and rubbed his chin. 'She told me she was in Leeds on holiday. Of course, that was rubbish. What did you find out? You had two days and two hundred quid. What have you got for the poor taxpayer?'

'I don't know what she was up to. She was always on the phone.'

'What was she saying? Who was she speaking to?'

'She was speaking Polish or German or something to somebody called Peter. Always seemed very earnest. But I couldn't understand a word.'

Angel pulled a face. 'Peter? Hmmm. Did she have her own car?'

'No, sir.'

'Did you try the taxi rank outside the hotel?'

'Yes, sir. No joy. Nobody will own up to taking her anywhere.'

Angel rubbed a hand across his mouth.

'I got her prints. On a menu,' Crisp said brightly, putting the envelope on the desk. 'It's a glossy surface. Should get good pulls.'

Angel nodded. 'That's something, I suppose. Hand it to DS Taylor in SOCO on the way out.' Angel sighed.

'Do you think she sussed you out for a copper?'

'I was very careful. Shouldn't have thought so.'

'Hmmm. Right. Well. We can't go chasing her up and down the country. There's something else come up. Richard Mace appears to have left his house. There are very few personal things left there. I want *you* to find him. You did the research on him. He's got to be somewhere.'

Crisp's jaw dropped. 'Where would I start, sir?' he asked pulling a long face and making cow eyes.

'You're a detective, aren't you? Quiz the postman and the milkman. Tour the garages. Get his car reg and you're on your way. Do you want me to do the bloody job for you?'

Crisp shook his head sullenly.

'You'll have to scratch about a bit,' Angel added. 'Go on. Get on with it then.'

Crisp slowly made for the door.

'And don't disappear into the Fat Duck,' Angel called after him. 'I like to see you now and again. I can just about tolerate you in small doses.'

The phone rang.

'I've got that call now to DI Elliott, sir.'

'Right, Ahmed. Thank you. Put him on,' Angel replied. 'Hello, is that Matthew? I've located the Patina treasure, Matthew, and a lot of other works of art and antiques by the looks of it.'

'What?! That's fantastic, Michael! Whereabouts?'

'In a private house. The owner of which is a Richard Mace. The one I was telling you about, here in Bromersley. I eventually managed to get inside. He has a big house and it's bursting with precious works of art, marble statues, paintings, Persian carpets and who knows what else. I've got the place guarded by uniformed. It will be covered morning, noon and night, but I'd be happy to pass it over to you. I can't afford to have men tied up on security work.'

'That's fantastic. I'll come up myself straight away and I'll have a squad up tomorrow. How on earth do you imagine this man Richard Mace came by all that stuff?'

'I've been working on that. Remember you told me that the last trace you had been able to make was of two men transporting the treasure through Sheffield on the first night of the blitz? And that your investigation came to an end with the notebook report of a Sheffield PC Shaw, I think his name was, who directed the RASC officer out of Sheffield onto the Bromersley Road?'

'Yes. Shaw in his report wrote that the officer's name was Captain Mecca.'

'Yes, and he must have written that down in the street when bombs were dropping all round him.'

'Yes.'

'Well, it occurred to me that the name he wrote actually was Captain Mace.'

'Hmmm. Of course,' Elliott said elatedly.

'So, I contacted War Office Records and found out that there was a Captain Stewart Mace in the RASC who was lost, presumed dead, in January 1941. But he didn't die: he went AWOL. The date fitted perfectly. I also learned that he was born in London in 1915. Now, he could have married and had a son around 1950, who would be around fifty-seven now. And that that would fit our man, Richard Mace.'

'That's great, Michael. I don't know how you do it.'

'I expect what happened was that the truck may have been damaged when they suffered the blast of a bombed building or when bouncing over the rubble and that they limped as far as Bromersley where they may have tried to phone their unit in London but couldn't get through.

London had also suffered excessive bomb damage around that time and lines were probably down. They were stranded, found lodgings or somewhere to stay. Hadn't much money, no ration books or petrol coupons. All they had was what was in the packing cases. Maybe the driver was killed or went AWOL. Anyway, Mace must have lived out the war around here, and after the war got married, had a son, Richard, and continued hanging onto the Patina treasure and adding to it. He was never found out until that girl stole probably the least valuable item, a candle-snuffer, from his fantastic hoard.'

Elliott said, 'Sounds logical to me. You know, Michael, you never cease to amaze me. Tell me. Among the spoils, are there any paintings of fat women with bare backsides?'

'A couple, I think.'

'Oh, Lord Truscott will be pleased. They'll likely be the two stolen from Truscott Priory last July. Worth millions. He'll be over the moon.'

'Yes, Angel. Come in,' Harker bellowed. 'What's this requisition for a new shirt and tie for PC Ahaz?' he snarled, waving the pink expense chitty.

Angel wasn't expecting any further argument about it.

'I had to make up a dummy parcel for Jondorf to reel in, sir. So I got the idea of improvising with a shirt and a tie.'

Harker frowned and put his hand to his forehead. 'You're making it up as you go along,' he said and stared at him with the look of a sanitary inspector looking into the cesspit in Dartmoor. 'You've been in the force that long, Angel, you think you know how to manipulate the facts to beat the system. But I'm afraid you can't get away with it, not while I'm in this chair anyway.'

'No, sir. It's not like that. The claim *is* valid. The explanation, as unlikely as it might seem, is absolutely true. It was the only way I could think of at the time. And we did get Ahaz back unharmed, and Jondorf and Schuster on remand. And we didn't call the Wakefield armed unit out. That would have cost a few hundred quid. There were no fees at all to pay out for externals. No extras. The entire operation was managed internally.'

Harker wrinkled the misshapen potato in the middle of his face that passed for his nose, and rubbed his mean, bony little chin. After a few moments, he sighed. 'Very well. I think I must be going soft,' he growled, then he signed the slip and tossed it into his out tray.

Angel looked on with unspoken satisfaction.

'How's Crisp doing with that undercover surveillance of that foreign woman?'

'He was doing very well, sir. However, she walked out of the hotel early this morning and disappeared.'

Harker sniffed. 'He couldn't hang onto the string on a kid's kite.'

'I interviewed her yesterday,' Angel continued. 'I don't think she's a suspect in the Johannson murder. She certainly knew the man, and she didn't like him, but then again, nobody did. However I do believe she is concerned in some way in the missing Patina Cathedral treasure.'

'You've got to kick him about a bit,' Harker snarled. 'Get your money's worth.'

Angel lifted his head and frowned. 'What?'

'It's the only way to get any work out of him. And get him to use his initiative.'

Angel blinked. 'Who?'

'Crisp of course! Who the hell do you think I'm talking about? He couldn't wipe his backside without a map.'

THIRTEEN

'DS Gawber left this copy of the list of telephone calls charged to Mark Johannson's suite while he was staying at the Imperial Grand Hotel, Leeds, sir. It comes to over £400. He was only there four nights. He was murdered on the fifth night.'

'Yes. Yes,' Angel said testily. 'Have you been through them?'

'They were all calls abroad, sir,' Ahmed said. 'The same number. Euromagna's studio in Burbank, California. And two to Norway.'

'Norway?' Angel said. 'I suppose he was Norwegian with a name like that?'

'Yes, sir. He was calling his mother.'

'Anywhere else?'

'No, sir.'

Angel sniffed. 'That doesn't move us ahead at all, does it?'

The phone rang. Angel looked across and reached out for it. The switchboard operator told him it was a Detective Sergeant Hooper from the Thames River Patrol, Metropolitan Police. Angel wondered who he was.

'Put him through.'

The man spoke with a tough, cockney accent. 'Do you know a man, Richard Mace, sir? His address is believed to be 2 Creeford Road, Bromersley. Six foot tall, black hair, suit, collar, tie.'

Angel frowned. He wondered whatever was coming next. 'I know *of* him, Sergeant, why?'

'Pulled his body out of the river by Waterloo Bridge, sir, two hours ago. Six bullets in his back. Got his address out of his wallet. Not robbery, though. He'd a pocket full of money, twenties and fifties, nearly four grand. He was also carrying a pistol. A Walther PPK with a full cartridge.'

Angel frowned.

'Anything known, sir?' Hooper added. 'He's not on the NPC. He's from round your way. I've got to put something on the docket.'

'Don't know much about him, Sergeant. He's not wanted by us for murder, but we have reason to believe he had been a big time thief of antiques and works of art. How long had he been in the water?'

'About a day, I'd say. Do you happen to know his next of kin, sir?'

'No.'

'There's a photograph of a girl in his pocket. Could be a daughter, or wife. And a sort of passport photograph of a man.'

'They mean nothing to me.'

Hooper sounded exasperated. 'Don't you want him, sir?'

Angel sighed. 'There isn't much percentage in a dead thief, Sergeant. He can't talk. He can't give evidence. He won't be a witness. And society won't be improved by locking him up.'

'Any idea who could have murdered him?'

'Six bullets in the back? Oh yes, I know exactly who murdered him. But you'll never catch him and you'll never prove it.'

'Isn't much use me trying then, is there, sir?'

Angel didn't reply. He was thinking how sad it was.

Hooper sighed. 'Come on, sir. Help me out. What'll I do with him?'

'If it was me,' Angel said. 'I'd put him in a box and send him carriage forward to lawyer, Peter Meissen, Westlenska, Patina, in the West Balkans. He'll be responsible.'

'You think it's a foreign job, sir?'

'I'm certain of it, Sergeant.'

Hooper sighed. 'Right, sir. Thank you. I'll try and push it onto Interpol, sir.'

'In this instance, Sergeant, they're the best people to deal with it.' Angel replaced the phone.

Ahmed was biting his lip. He looked down at Angel. 'Another murder, sir?'

'Yes, lad.'

'How did you know it was Peter Meissen who was responsible, sir?'

'There was £4000 in his pocket. If you were a crook would you have left it there?'

'I suppose not.'

'Meissen was not a thief. Also, six shots in the back. One shot would have been enough. Anymore than two would be excessive. Six was blatantly callous. The murder was political. The executioner wanted to show how ruthless and thorough he could be.'

Ahmed shuddered. 'Like, keep your hands off our treasures?'

'Exactly.'

It was about an hour later when the phone rang again. He grabbed it. 'Angel.'

'DS Taylor, sir, SOCO. We had a hotel menu handed in this morning by Trevor Crisp. You wanted prints taking off it. He said they were of a woman, name of Flavia Radowitz. Very small fingers.'

'Yes, that's right, Don.'

'Well, sir, we've found comparison prints … her thumb, first and second fingers of her right hand are on a silver candlestick that was in the main room at Number 2, Creeford Road.'

Angel looked up and his mouth dropped open. So, Flavia Radowitz had been in that house. That was unexpected. Very unexpected.

'Did you get that, sir?' Taylor said.

'Yes. Yes. Thank you, Don. I was thinking.'

'I thought you'd like to know.'

'Yes. Thank you, Don. Great stuff. Did you come across anything else of interest in Creeford Road?'

'Oh yes, sir. Everything. It's all truly magnificent. I've never seen anything like it.'

He smiled. 'I meant forensically?'

'Oh? No, sir. Nothing of interest. Lots of prints from a largish hand, probably all the same man.'

'Right, Don. Thank you.' He replaced the phone, pushed the swivel chair back and gazed up at the ceiling. He rubbed his earlobe. He wondered how Flavia Radowitz's prints could have appeared in Number 2, Creeford Road. It was a surprise, but fingerprints don't lie.

There was a knock at the door.

'Come in!'

It was Gawber, waving his notebook at Angel.

'Just the man,' Angel said. 'Richard Mace's body has been pulled out of the Thames.'

Gawber nodded. 'Ahmed told me, sir,' he said grimly. 'No less than he deserves.'

Angel sighed. 'You can call off the searches into his background. We know enough and we can't prosecute him or Peter Meissen. He'll be safely back in Patina by now. That's up to Interpol. Let them earn their keep.'

Gawber nodded in agreement.

'Now what did you want, Ron?' Angel said pointing to a chair.

'I managed to get back to the Johannson murder enquiry, sir. You asked me to see what I could find out about Otis Stroom and Harry Lee, sir. And it's not much.'

'Go on,' Angel said.

Gawber sat down and immediately started coughing. 'Sorry, sir.' He continued coughing. He took the bottle of cough mixture out of his pocket. 'Excuse me.' He took a sip. The coughing stopped.

'I thought you'd got over that. Why don't you go to the doctor's? That stuff will burn your throat out. I told you it contains arsenic.'

'I'm getting better, sir.'

'You must have a cupboard full of it.'

'It works, sir. It stops me coughing,' he said as put he put the bottle back in his pocket.'

Angel said, 'If it were mine, I'd find a better use for it than burning my throat out. Go on, then.'

'Well, sir, Stroom was born in Lancaster in 1970. Christened John Stroom. Only child of the Stroom family, small mill owners, who made ribbon. His father and mother are still there. They closed production down a few years ago, and are now importing it from China. Otis went to the local school then to a private stage school run by an old woman called Madame Polta in Manchester. His good looks and strong voice got him parts in theatre, then telly, then films. Made a few very famous films in the States as well as here. Married once. Didn't take. Lasted a year. Now single. Earns a lot of money. Endorses "Kisstingle toothpaste, the toothpaste for men that makes all the girls say yes." You must have heard of it, sir. The jingle drives me bats.'

Angel smiled. 'Any more?'

'A bit. Lives in a chalet in Switzerland. Doesn't drink. Not teetotal, but not known to drink much. Not known to be a member of any clubs, well, posh clubs; the ones I asked wouldn't tell me whether he was or not. And there's nothing known about him on the PNC. That's it for Stroom, sir.'

Angel wrinkled his nose. 'What does he do for crumpet?'

'Nothing as far as I can see. He's not known for chasing it, sir. No need to. It chases *him* all the time. But he likes to have something tasty on his arm at film premieres and red-carpet jobs.'

Angel nodded, but then began to rub his chin. Gawber's answer didn't quite satisfy him. 'What about Harry Lee?'

'He's obviously of Chinese descent, but he's American. Born in Seattle in 1958. Married an American woman. Three kids. Lives over there on the west coast. Works mainly for studios in Hollywood. He travels for the big money. Regarded in film circles as one of the world's best cameramen. Doesn't socialize. Keeps himself to himself. Seems to be the essence of respectability.'

Angel pulled a face. Anyone described as the essence of respectability probably wasn't. Like those clean-cut, professional charmers in the entertainment business and politics who claim to be 'born again Christians'. In his experience, everyone who had ever made that claim, always turned out to be a conman or a thief, or both. 'By their fruits shall ye know them', was the only dependable way of judging the worthiness of a man, Angel reckoned, but he never talked about it. There was a knock at the door. It was Ahmed. He came in, all smiles. 'I've been in touch with the credit card office of the Northern Bank, sir.'

'Aye? That tramp, lad. What about him?'

'The man, Alexander Bernedetti is well respected by the bank, sir. His credit history is excellent. He's got one of what they call a diamond card. Only given to the very rich. They couldn't give me a physical description of him because, of course, they don't know him. His regular account is held at their branch in High Holborn. So I went through to them. One of the tellers said he was about fifty, average height, well built but not fat, dark hair, greying.'

Angel nodded. 'That fits. So far.'

Ahmed said, 'They believe he is an actor. Very successful. Something to do with Euromagna, and—'

'Euromagna!' Angel said screwing up his face. 'That's the outfit that's making that film up at Tunistone that

Johannson was directing.' The wheels and cogs in his mind began to whiz round.

'Alexander Bernedetti?' Gawber said slowly. 'Oh yes. It's a famous name in the film world. Just remembered. I think he was supposed to be in the cast of the film they're making up there: the biography of Edgar Poole.'

'Then what's he doing dead, in tramp's clothes, with a sovereign in his mouth, and a diamond credit card sewn into his coat?'

The phone rang again. It was a few minutes before 5.00 p.m.

The civilian on the station switchboard said that it was a Sister Josephson from the Bromersley General Hospital asking to speak to him.

Angel frowned. He didn't know her and he wasn't aware that anyone he knew was in hospital.

'I have a patient here, Inspector,' Sister Josephson explained. 'Admitted last night. He's quite poorly. Appears to have been living on the streets. We've done the best we can with him. I'm afraid he could still be cleaner. Had to put him in a room on his own. Anyway, he says he has no next of kin and, I must say, nobody has been asking after him. Not had any visitors, and he's asking for you. His name is Harry Hull. Says you know him. Says he has something very important to tell you.'

Angel rubbed his mouth. That was unusual. He knew Harry Hull very well. He was a small-time burglar. He had been in trouble most of the time Angel had been on the force, and had been in and out of prison frequently. Angel had been responsible for sending him there on some of those occasions. He couldn't imagine why he should be asking for him. He couldn't understand why Hull was living the life of a man on the road either. The last time Angel had anything to do with him, he was married and had two sons grown-up sons.

'Yes, I know him, Sister,' he said unemotionally.

'Sounds important, Inspector,' she replied. 'If you are able speak to him, I should come as soon as you can. He is on ward eleven. You can visit any time.'

'Thank you, Sister,' Angel said, and he slowly replaced the phone in the cradle. Her last few words lingered in his mind. She had made it sound as if Hull wasn't here for long. The call had come at a very inconvenient time. He was up to his neck in two nasty murders and a very strange robbery. He really hadn't the time to be running after a ten-a-penny tea leaf.

He went through the door marked 'ward eleven', spotted the nurses' station and went up to it. The nurse looked up.

'I've come to see a man called Hull, Harry Hull,' Angel said. 'Sister Josephson said—'

'You must be Inspector Angel? He's asking for you, but don't stay too long. Don't tire him.'

'What's the matter with him?'

'He needs a lot of rest,' she said vaguely in the best tradition of the medical profession.

Angel took it to mean, 'We are not telling you, so do what you have to do, quietly, then go away.'

'He's in there,' she added, pointing to an open door just behind him.

'Thank you,' he said. He turned round, went across the corridor to the doorway and peered inside the little room.

There was a small man with long hair, a beard and a moustache in a bed. He had wires, pipes and tubes leading away from various orifices and places. At the head of the bed was an illuminated screen with a graph and markers and numbers, which changed regularly to the rhythmical accompaniment of a bleeping sound. The wall facing the door was made of glass and looked over the town of Bromersley. Opposite that was a wall-fitted hand basin and in the corner stood a chair.

Angel reached out for the chair, pulled it to the side of the bed, sat down and looked at the whiskered man. His eyes were closed and he seemed to be asleep. His face and stringy neck were red and chapped, the result of the English winter. He bore only the slightest resemblance to the Harry

Hull that he had frequently hunted, caught and sometimes charged over the twenty-four years he had been on the force.

Hull made a slight movement, cleared his throat and then slowly opened his eyes. He saw the big face of somebody looking at him. He blinked and rubbed his eyes with clenched fists, then looked again.

'It's you. Dear old Inspector Angel,' he said hoarsely in a voice that sounded as if he'd been gargling on petrol.

Angel looked down at him. 'You asked to see me, Harry,' he said with a snigger. 'The very first time in your life *you* actually asked to see *me*.'

Hull managed a brief smile. It quickly left him. 'You'll be surprised to see me in here, Inspector … like this?'

Angel nodded his head slightly.

Hull hunched up the bed a little and said, 'You haven't got a ciggie on you, have you?'

'No.'

Hull looked disappointed but not surprised. 'The truth is, Mr Angel, Marlene walked out on me. After twenty-eight years of happy married life. I can't understand it.'

Angel knew his history. He could easily understand it. He shook his head wryly.

'I got back to my house after that stretch in Durham,' Hull continued. 'I had only served eight months of it. When I got back to the house, it was filled with strangers. *Strangers*! They told me they'd been there *three* months. No Marlene. All my stuff gone. No clothes. Nothing. No forwarding address. Went round the Probation. They fixed me up with temporary bed and breakfast. But that was no good.'

'You've two sons, haven't you?'

He pulled an unhappy face. 'Don't know where they are. Been gone eight years. Both married. Got kids of their own now. They pushed off after the newspapers printed that photograph of me with that model who was found dead in Big John Lucas's swimming pool.'

Angel remembered it and nodded.

'But I was found not guilty of any wrongdoing by a jury and Judge Casilis, Mr Angel. You know that! It was all written up in the newspapers. I told them that, but they didn't believe me. I haven't seen either of them since.'

Angel felt sorry for the man but was determined not to get involved with his domestic relationships. 'What did you want with me, Harry? I tell you, I'm no use at marriage guidance. Or "Happy Families".'

'No,' he said grimly. 'I know. I'm not going there, Mr Angel. I know what you're best at, and I think I can help you.'

Angel raised his head. This wasn't the Harry Hull he had grown to know, dislike and distrust over the years. He frowned as he thought about it. 'Not going straight, at last, Harry?' he said wryly. 'Now why would you want to do that?'

'Look at me, Mr Angel. Do I look as if I'm about to go out and do a bank job or something? Nah. I've run out of choices. And I've run out of steam. I'm nearly at the end of the line. I'm going to be lucky to get out of this butcher's shop alive.' He shuddered as he spoke those words. He wiped his nose on the pyjama jacket sleeve and then continued. 'And if I do, what am I going to be fit enough to do? Weave a few baskets for the hospice for a month or two? Nah. I know the score. Before I go, I might as well try and earn a few merit marks … from him up there.' He glanced momentarily up at the ceiling. 'Besides there's nobody else I can tell, is there? And although I reckon you've cost me about eight years liberty during my life, I've deserved it, and you've always been fair and given the evidence as it was and not exaggerated anything. And when that smart-arse barrister tried to get me on fencing as well as burgling, you got that charge of fencing dismissed, because you knew it was Dollie Reuben. That saved me an extra two years in the pokey.'

Angel realized that Hull must have something really significant to say. 'What is it, Harry? Are you going to come to the point?'

'Yes. Sure. Well, the thing is, about a week or ten days ago, I can't exactly remember which day. It was about six o'clock in the evening, I suppose. It was pitch black, I knows that, and I was knackered. I wasn't well. I was full of cold. I was trying to get tolerably comfortable to rest under the railway arches on Wath Road with a half bottle of rum. I'd got one of those thick cardboard boxes, so I was well off the cold concrete. There were four others sheltering in there under the arches. Five of us altogether. Sammy the smell, Dennis the drunk, the Professor and the Duke. We'd settled down for a spell, when a flash car pulls up on the pavement. I couldn't see it, but I could tell by the sound it was posh. The sound of the brakes, the hum of the engine, the clunk of the door as it shut. I saw the shadow of a man put his head through one of the arches. He come through, waving a flashlight about. Well, of course Sammy, Dennis and the Professor takes up and leaves straight away. Men of the road don't like light, where it's meant to be dark, Mr Angel. I was hid away behind and leaning up against a pillar, and I was dead beat. If you gets there early, you can get a pillar. I was too ill. I'd taken a few sleepers and had a slug or two of black rum. I wasn't in no state to be beetling off to look for a new hole to rest in, so I stayed. I snuggled down a bit and didn't move. I knew that the Duke knew I was there, but he seemed to be decent enough. He wouldn't do me no harm. The man called out a name – Alex, I think. The Duke answered him. He didn't seem pleased to see him. I think maybe you chaps were after him. He was on about the posh man breaking his cover. I wondered if he was a copper. The posh man said something about pulling out of the Agapoo project and that if he did, he'd give him half a million quid. The Duke said no. Straight away. I couldn't believe it. There he was, on the bones of his arse, refusing an offer of half a million quid! He said he could pretend to be ill or something, or go off his rocker, anything that would stop the Agapoo, whatever it was, from going ahead. Anyway, Duke says no. But the man couldn't believe it. He said he'd get more for throwing a sickie than he would for completing the whole project, and he'd have to do nothing for it. The posh man said he could easily find a quack to certify his illness was genuine. The Duke got angry. He didn't like the man, his idea, his Agapoo or nothing. He told him to sod off. The posh bloke tried to smarm round him, said that only he could help him out, that he had serious woman trouble.' Hull grinned. 'Who hasn't?'

'Did he say her name?'

'No. Not as I can remember. Anyway, the Duke told him to push off, that *he* was risking blowing his cover. The posh man was all worked up. He said he was at the end of his tether, that he owed him a favour and that if he wouldn't pull out, voluntary like, he'd have to assist him. The Duke said in what way? This way, the man said and then I heard two gun shots, and I saw the flashes. In that place, they were very loud. Echoed round them arches something frightening. I thought my heart was going to jump out of my body. It shook me rigid, I can tell you. I dared not move, couldn't risk being seen by him. I froze on the spot, pulled a rag over my face, slid down inside my overcoat and concentrated on breathing silently. I was afraid my hooky chest might give me away. But the man then ran straight out of the arches. I heard the car start up and race away. I lay there shivering. I was too afraid to do anything for a bit. Nobody came, so after a while, I crawled over to where the Duke was. I called his name, shook him. But I knew he was dead. I went through his pockets for any smokes or money. There was about a hundred quid, a pen knife, a tube of mints and a handkerchief. That's all. I took them. I don't mind telling you. If I hadn't, the next man on the road would have frisked him clean, so might as well have been me.'

Hull stopped. He leaned over to the locker at the side of the bed. A skinny hand slipped out through a wide pyjama sleeve and picked up a plastic glass. He took a sip of water.

Angel said, 'Is that it? Is that *all* you wanted to tell me, Harry?'

'I gave him something back,' he said, replacing the glass with a shaking hand.

'What was that?'

'I had a gold sovereign in my sock. I kept it for when I thought my number was up. I put it in his mouth to pay his way over the Styx. Which reminds me. I hope I recovers out of here, so that I can get myself another sov for when I breathes my last.'

Angel rubbed his chin and looked into Hull's watery eyes. He was thinking. For once, one of Harry Hull's stories had the ring of truth about it. There were one or two things he wasn't quite sure about though.

'The man with the gun called the Duke Alex?'

'Yes.'

'But Alex or the Duke didn't address him by any name at all?'

'No.'

'They obviously knew each other very well?'

'Oh yes.'

'His voice. What sort of an accent was there?'

'No accent. Well spoken. Posh even. That's all I can say about it.'

'And what was this Agapoo?'

Hull shook his head. 'No idea, Mr Angel. No idea.'

FOURTEEN

'Good morning, sir,' Angel said as he closed the door. 'You wanted me?'

Harker was seated behind his desk. He looked as miserable as a man with toothache sitting in the waiting room at the Inland Revenue. 'Aye. Sit down. One or two things. How are you getting along with the tramp murder?'

'Haven't had a chance to write up my report on that, sir. There were a few developments yesterday. The so-called tramp turns out to be a very successful actor and a bit of a leading light in the film world. His name was Alexander Bernedetti.'

Harker wrinkled his nose. 'Name sounds familiar. What was *he* doing squatting in the arches?'

'Maybe he was down on his luck.'

'Or taken to the bottle.'

'We have a witness who overheard the actual murder.'

'But didn't see it, I suppose?'

'No sir. An interesting fact has come up. Bernedetti was in the cast of the same film Johannson was working on.'

'Two men in the same film shot dead?'

'And it looks like the same MO, sir.'

'What did you get from the witness?'

'Only that the man who shot the victim was male, well spoken, drives an expensive car, knew the victim well enough to call him Alex, and seemed to be in a gang or something referred to as "Agapoo".'

'Agapoo? Nonsense. Doesn't make sense.' Harker did his impression of an orangutan and then said, 'And what about Johannson's murderer? Who do you suspect? Whoever you suspect of the one murder, may have committed the second.'

'Yes, indeed, sir. Well, nobody seems to have liked Johannson. The people who have no alibis are Otis Stroom and Harry Lee.'

'The actor, Otis Stroom, I remember. Very famous. Who is this Harry Lee?'

'American cameraman. Highly rated in the film world.'

'What about the actress's boyfriend, Hugo Moss.'

'He's too lightweight, sir. Besides, he has an alibi. He was with Nanette Quadrette all night.'

'So she says,' he said heavily.

Angel nodded in agreement.

'Well, it's high time you had a firm line of enquiry,' he said, then he added, 'Mmm. Very well. I'll let you get back to it.'

Angel stood up.

Then Harker said, 'Ah,' as he suddenly remembered something. 'Where is it?' He leaned forward and ferreted in a wire basket on his desk. He eventually found a pink expense voucher. He looked at it again. His mood changed. He began waving the paper about. 'What the dickens is this £200 about?' he said.

Angel knew exactly what it was, even though it was being fluttered over the desk like a Union Jack at the Queen's visit. 'It's what I paid out to DS Crisp for him to entertain Flavia Radowitz to try to obtain information about her relationship with the victim, Mark Johannson, sir. If you remember, she was seen going to his room on two occasions shortly before his murder.'

Harker sniffed. 'And what did he find out?'

'As it happened, the explanations she gave me were subsequently proved to be true and wholly innocent.'

'I asked, what did *he* find out?'

Angel had to think quickly. 'Crisp softened her up for my interview where she said that she discovered that Johannson only fancied her and was trying to get … friendly.'

Harker nodded knowingly. 'I thought so. Crisp didn't find out *anything*. So you didn't get any hard evidence about the murderer of Johannson from her?'

'He covertly obtained her fingerprints. Fingerprints that have turned up on a candlestick in Mace's house.'

Harker blinked. 'Whatever was she doing in Mace's house?' Before Angel could answer, he added, 'But the fact is that the money Crisp spent on wining and dining this woman didn't actually move the case one inch forward.'

Angel could see he was losing the argument. 'Well he got the fingerprints, sir.'

'You could have obtained those any time, either covertly or formally. I can't see that, in this case, it would have made the slightest difference. No, I can't pass this,' he said tossing the expense chit to the waste-paper basket.

Angel's jaw tightened. He breathed in deeply and said, 'You can't refuse to sanction a legitimate expense on the basis that it added little or nothing to an investigation, sir. If that were to happen, we'd never be able even to risk going out on any cold investigative interview that might not produce a positive result.'

Harker wrinkled his nose. His chalk-like complexion reddened at the top of his cheeks.

'In this instance, I can and I do. I wouldn't normally demean myself with an explanation, but I give my reasons. Firstly, the money was actually spent on food and drink, in other words, somebody, in this case Crisp, had some actual benefit out of it. Knowing Crisp, it was probably ninety per cent drink, and flowing his way. Secondly, I was not consulted in this matter, and I know that you are well aware that when it comes to spending public money on matters over and above the delineated budget, it requires special sanction. I wasn't consulted. And furthermore, if I had been consulted I would not have given it.'

Angel came out of Harker's office steaming with rage. He charged up the green corridor to his own office and banged shut the door. He was smarting about the injustice of it all and wondered how on earth he was supposed to make up the shortfall of £200? He couldn't possibly expect Crisp to share in the loss. Angel had supplied the money directly to him and he would have thought he was spending legitimate police funds. He couldn't be expected to have to pay it back. There was no comeback there. Angel thought that he might consider applying to the Federation; however, Harker was technically within his rights to withhold reimbursing him because he had not authorized the payment of it in the first place. It particularly rankled with Angel, because in his experience, officers of his rank were always entrusted to make sensible decisions about expenditure in the course of their work. There might be some disagreement afterwards about the rightness or wrongness of the decision to incur the expense, but reimbursement was always made. He must be sure that Mary didn't hear about this; she might come up here and box Horace Harker's ears.

He settled down after a few minutes and began tapping out his report on his laptop. This was soon done and then he began to wade through the accumulation of post. His first filter through, he could do at speed; the second filter through was slower; the third filter required some thought. He stopped at that, pushed back the chair and looked up at the ceiling.

'Agapoo,' he said. Then again, 'Agapoo.' He said the word loudly, quietly, slowly, then quickly. He spoke it in all the accents he knew, broad Yorkshire, Scottish, Irish, scouse, cockney, American and pseudo French, German and Italian. He said it distinctly and then, putting his hand across his mouth to muffle the sound, indistinctly. And then suddenly he understood exactly what the word meant.

Angel drove the BMW through Bromersley town and onto the Tunistone road to the film location site. He turned off the main road, and, overtaking the horse and trap still waiting patiently on the rough track, drove the car into the field and parked it near Otis Stroom's luxury caravan.

He could see the film unit, lights, camera, cast and crew assembled round the farmhouse door and walked across the field down to them. It seemed that he had arrived at a significant moment.

Grant Montague, immaculately turned out, was standing on a trailer and addressing the cast and crew. By his side was Sean Tattersall. The crew were pressing close up to the trailer, silent and intent on hearing Montague's every word. Standing in the doorway of the farmhouse, head erect, was Otis Stroom, wearing black-rimmed spectacles; Nanette Quadrette, looking miserably beautiful as ever, was standing next to Hugo Moss, and on the camera dolly, was Harry Lee.

'I know, ladies and gentlemen, boys and girls,' Grant said, 'that this has been a trying time for you, as it has for me and I thank you for buckling down and helping me out as I have tried to keep the production of the film rolling. As you know, I intended to stand in as director only until we could get a top-notch man, a worthy successor to Mark Johannson. But I regret that, at such short notice, there are no film directors available who could undertake this mammoth job with the flair and panache it really requires. Now, this morning, I read in the papers – I expect you all did too – that Alexander Bernedetti has been found dead. He was to have played Edgar Poole's father, an important, character part, who, in his latter days finished up as a poor tramp. Perfectionist as he was, Mr Bernedetti had apparently adopted a tramp's disguise to get into the character of the role, but was mistaken for a real man of the road and was tragically murdered and robbed. There goes another great artist irreplaceable in the world of entertainment. I immediately consulted my fellow directors and they are of the opinion that it has now become impossible to continue to try to portray this great story on film at this time. As well as the casting difficulties, some artist's contracts would now run out before filming is completed, which would present more complications. Of course, this great biopic may be produced in the future, as Euromagna have bought exclusive rights to the screenplay. I don't know. Only the insurance company might know if and when this might be. If it was left to me, I would have tried to find a replacement film director and an actor for the role of Edgar Poole's father and pressed on. It wouldn't have been easy, but … there you are.'

There was unsettled muttering among the crew then Montague held up his hands to stop the chatter and said, 'All contracts, of course, will be honoured. Nobody will be out of pocket. Euromagna will meet all agreed liabilities and expenses. Send in your claims in writing to the London office and I will personally deal with them. Thank you everybody, so much, and I hope to have the pleasure of working with you all again some time in the future. Now, I will hand you over to Sean Tattersall to make the arrangements for the return of the unit to the studio in Buckinghamshire and the clearing of the site.'

There were mutters of discontent, then most of the crew crowded round Sean Tattersall.

With a sober face, Otis Stroom walked athletically up the field towards his caravan. Four teenage girls from Tunistone, who probably should have been in school, were swinging on a gate. They waved and screamed at him as he passed thirty yards away, but he was totally unaware of them, which made them scream all the more.

Behind Stroom came Nanette Quadrette, looking moodily magnificent. She was escorted by Hugo Moss and two women from wardrobe. They were making their way to her caravan, which was next door to Stroom. Quadrette strode elegantly passed the groupies with her nose in the air and her cloak flying. The girls' attitude to the actress was more of stunned amazement. They stared at her with eyes that stuck out like gobstoppers on sticks. They gasped, put their hands over their mouths and breathily said, 'My God, oh my God,' over and over again.

Montague stepped down from the trailer and Angel went up to him. He saw him and made a sad face.

Angel said, 'I just heard the news about closing the production of the film. I'm sorry to hear it.'

'Unavoidable, Inspector. Totally unavoidable. I would have carried on, but it was not viable. My American partners convinced me of it.'

'I didn't know that the late Alexander Bernedetti had been posing as a tramp for the purposes of preparing for a part in the film.'

'He was a method actor of great style, Inspector. He will be sadly missed.'

'Were you aware he was doing that, Mr Montague?'

'No, not at the time, but I am not a bit surprised. He was a stickler for detail.'

'Well, how did you find out?'

Montague frowned. 'Our press office knew all about it, apparently. It was good PR. How our leading character actor prepared himself for the part of Edgar Poole's father, and so on.'

Angel nodded. 'Yes, of course. One other thing, Mr Montague.'

'Yes?' he said impatiently. He seemed to be edging to get away.

Angel was undeterred. 'Who wins from the cancellation of the film?'

Montague pursed his lips and said, 'Nobody. Absolutely nobody, dear sir.'

'Do the principals get paid in full?'

'These matters are really quite confidential, Inspector,' Montague said.

'This is a murder enquiry, Mr Montague. Delicate points about money may be vital in determining matters of motive. Nothing can remain confidential, I assure you.'

His eyebrows shot up. 'Are you suggesting that one of our two principals is a murderer, Inspector?'

Angel looked closely at him and waited.

Montague nodded and said, 'Well, as a matter of fact, they each receive a proportion. Both Mr Stroom and Miss Quadrette will receive a quarter of the figure it was agreed each was to be paid for the complete film. It was to have taken thirteen weeks maximum, then no more than five days after that, by mutual arrangement, for publicity shots and retakes.'

'So, who wins on the cancellation of the film?' Angel persisted.

'Nobody wins.'

'Do the directors win?'

'How can they? The potential earnings of the biopic of this legendary man, with these three great stars, top director, top screenplay, Oscar-winning cinema photographer, were enormous. Millions! Now there will be nothing.'

'You are insured?'

'Yes. Sure thing, and committing the unique love story of the late Edgar Poole, a real celebrity, to film, with the talent we had lined up, while most of the facts and locations were still available to us, would have made the film a certain financial bonanza. A film of this calibre could still have been earning money sixty or seventy years from now. We are talking millions of pounds, Inspector. Twenty, fifty million pounds or even more. The compensation the insurance will pay out will in no way compare to the earnings this extravaganza would have made over the years.'

Angel nodded. He licked his lips. 'Well, thank you, Mr Montague. I must catch Otis Stroom before he leaves. Will you excuse me?' Angel strode over the field to Stroom's caravan.

The leading man had removed the tight black coat with ruffled collar and sleeves, discarded the hair pieces from his forehead and temples and was removing the tanned outdoor look from his handsome square-jawed face with cold cream and cotton wool.

'Come in, Inspector. I saw you back there. You will have heard the shocking news? Now that Alexander Bernedetti has been found dead, Grant Montague says that Euromagna is cancelling the film. Who is next, Inspector? Is the murderer going to polish off everybody connected with the enterprise? Is it somebody who doesn't want the story of the great man to be told? And if so, why?'

Angel shrugged. 'I think you are safe enough, Mr Stroom, now that the film is cancelled.'

'I certainly hope so. It wreaks havoc with my image. It does not suit me to be associated with anything that fails. I only want to be associated with success stories, if you see what I mean.'

Angel saw exactly what he meant, but he wasn't much impressed by it. 'You'll be handsomely paid for the short time that you have committed to the film, won't you?'

'If you consider it on a rate per hour basis, like a tradesman, of course. However if the film had been completed and promoted by Euromagna, it would have made a bomb, and, I would not only have received payment for making the film, but I would have earned a royalty every time the film was shown. It could have been considered as part of my pension. It may also have been a stepping stone to some even greater role. That will not happen now. In actual fact, for the first time in five years, I believe that I am actually out of work.'

Angel sighed. He felt sorry for him, but not a lot.

'You haven't been able to come up with any names or description of anybody you bumped into the evening Johannson was murdered, I suppose?'

'To be honest, Inspector, I haven't even tried. I told you. I was meandering round the streets of Leeds. The last thing I wanted was to be recognized.'

Angel sniffed. 'Well, Mr Stroom,' he said grimly. 'You've been remarkably successful in that regard. What about Tuesday night of 13 February, the night Alexander Bernedetti was murdered?'

'I have really no idea.'

Angel wrinkled his nose. 'Well, I should do what you can,' he said meaningfully.

Angel took his leave politely, and as he came down Stroom's caravan steps, he saw Harry Lee opening the boot of a big Mercedes he appeared to have hired from a London car hire firm.

'Glad I caught you, Mr Lee.'

The American looked up at him from the boot lid. He was packing a case containing valuable lenses, which only he chose to handle. 'Ah, Inspector Angel, isn't it?'

Angel smiled. 'I wanted to check on a few things.'

'Oh? Yes?'

'You knew Alexander Bernedetti?'

'Oh yes, of course. I had the pleasure of working with him on several films. A good, square jaw, easy to light, whether as a hero or a villain. One of the world's natural charmers. Very tragic, his murder.'

'He was a friend of yours?'

'Oh no. But he was a friendly and unassuming man.'

Angel pursed his lips. 'Unfortunately, you were unable to supply an alibi for the time of the death of Mark Johannson. Can you provide me with an alibi for the time of the death of Mr Bernedetti? He was shot in Wath Road railway arches, in Bromersley on the evening of 13 February.'

'I would have to think about that, Inspector.'

'You'd better think about it quickly, Mr Lee. Here's my card. Perhaps you'll let me know. Somebody wanted to stop the making of this film. Whoever that is, is also the murderer of two men. That murderer could be you. If it is not you, take it from me, it's someone you know very well indeed.'

FIFTEEN

Hugo Moss answered the caravan door. He had a large comb in his hand.

'I want to speak to Miss Nanette Quadrette,' Angel said.

Moss looked back into the van. 'It's that copper again, Nan. You haven't time to thee him, have you?'

Angel blinked. His jaw tightened. 'She certainly has, lad,' he growled. 'This is not a social call,' he added as he pushed Moss aside with one hand and stepped inside the caravan. 'I haven't popped round to show you my holiday snaps on the beach at Filey. I'm investigating the murder of two men.' Angel looked for her through the forest of flowers.

Moss followed him in. 'You can't thee her, the's not dressed!'

She was sitting at a dressing table facing a mirror surrounded by lights. She was wearing something short and white with straps over her thin brown shoulders.

Quadrette saw him and screamed. Angel looked away. It wasn't a scream of embarrassment. She was wild with anger.

'There is no need to push your way in, Inthpector,' Moss said.

'What's the meaning of this?' she snapped, as she reached out for a long white housecoat on the bed behind her.

Angel swallowed quickly in exasperation. 'I can't have your pet monkey messing me around, lady!'

Moss breathed in deeply and glared at him.

Angel looked round at Quadrette who was now covered from her neck to her ankles in white towelling.

'I am looking into a double murder,' he said. 'And I have some very serious questions to put to you.'

She tied the cord of the housecoat, settled herself back in front of the mirror again and snatched up a hairbrush. 'I've had a very gruelling day, Inspector,' she whined.

Moss gently took the hairbrush from her and began brushing her long black hair with long, soft strokes.

'I don't know if I'm up to answering questions,' she said. 'The bloody film is cancelled. My plans are up in the air. I don't know what I am going to do now. It's that bastard Grant Montague; he's had it in for me for years. I had originally planned to have a year off, but I have nowhere decent to go. The house in the Maldives has been sold. Hugo has already said that he was willing to accept the offer from the Pizziano chain for his three salons to buy a villa on Koz for us.'

Angel's mouth tightened.

'I don't expect Cheetah,' he said, glancing at Moss, 'was anywhere near you the night that Mark Johannson was murdered, was he?'

'Yeth, I was. All night. Every minute of it,' Moss said.

'He was,' she confirmed firmly.

Angel looked at Moss and said, 'And where were you the night of Tuesday, 13 February? That was the night of the murder of Alexander Bernedetti.'

Hugo Moss stopped brushing Quadrette's hair. His jaw dropped open. 'If you think I could possibly murder anybody, you must be potty.'

'It's true,' Quadrette said. 'He's far too sensitive.'

Angel wasn't easily put off. 'Well, *where* were you?' he growled

Moss curled his lip like a petulant schoolboy. 'I don't know, do I? I don't keep a diary or anything. I haven't the time.'

Angel sniffed. 'You might wish you had.'

'It couldn't have been him,' Quadrette said. 'He couldn't harm a fly.'

Despite what she said, Angel could visualize him pulling wings off a fly one at a time and enjoying it. He glared at Moss and then at Quadrette and took a stab in the dark.

'I've a good mind to arrest you for withholding information,' he said boldly.

Moss stared back at him. His bottom lip trembled. Angel saw Quadrette shudder.

There was a pause, she sighed, took a deep breath, and said, 'All right, Mr Angel. So you know about Grant Montague and me. But it has nothing at all to do with these murders. Absolutely nothing. I assure you.'

Angel was pleased the gamble had paid off, but he didn't show it.

'You don't have to admit to anything, Nan,' Moss said. 'If you don't want to.'

Angel glared at him. 'If you don't shut this gibbering monkey up, I will take him outside and strap him to a tree or something,' he shouted.

Quadrette looked with pained eyes at the young man who lowered his head. With a quick jerk of her hand she pointed to the bed. He pulled a disagreeable face, tossed the hairbrush onto the dressing table, moved over to the bed, flopped onto it, kicked off his shoes and lounged on it, one arm propping up his head. His nose was turned up, his wet mouth hanging open as he looked at her.

'You say it has nothing *directly* to do with the murders. Maybe, but I'd like to hear *your* version of events. When did this all start?' Angel said, cunningly.

'I assure you, Inspector, it has nothing at all to do with the murders, *nothing*. I never thought he would have told you anything at all about it. It was after I left RADA. I went round all the agencies and simply couldn't get work. I heard that Euromagna were looking to cast *The Fly That Got Away* so I applied. Saw him there and I stupidly told him I was desperate, so he got me work temporarily at the escort agency he runs with Violet Buhl.' She broke off. 'But he will have told you all this?'

Angel nodded. 'He told me *that* much,' he lied. 'And he said that you got the part in *The Fly That Got Away*,' Angel added. He had remembered that from the mammoth publicity drive at the time of the launch of the film.

'That was my first break,' she said brightly. 'Never looked back since. Snapped up to make four films for The Ciro Corporation, and then came back home to do this damned thing.' Then she wrinkled her nose, looked coyly at Angel and said, 'I hope it won't have to get out to the media, how I got started.'

'I shouldn't think so,' he said.

'Lots of well-known actors have to struggle at the beginning. Even that idiot Otis Stroom was on their books for a while, you know.'

Angel blinked when he heard her mention Stroom's name. He looked into her eyes thoughtfully. 'What's the address of that escort agency?'

Angel dashed back to his office and closeted himself in there for the rest of the afternoon. He made several phone calls, carefully recording them on tape. At 5.00 p.m. he closed his office and went home; it was Friday and he was thankful of it. He took the tapes home and played them several times on his own tape deck. On Saturday morning, he mooned around the garden, casually, lazily pulling up a winter weed or two but not attacking the flower borders at all seriously.

Mary knew something was bothering him. By Saturday evening, she said, 'Michael. You must relax. I know it's that murder case that's on your mind, but you must stop thinking about it. Now, relax and watch the television with me. You know full well, if you stop thinking about it, the answer, or whatever it is, will come to you.'

He nodded. She was absolutely right. 'Yes, all right,' he said and carried on thinking about it.

It was when they were watching highlights of selections of repeats, of clips of extracts, taken from excerpts, from past series of *Only Fools and Horses* that Angel suddenly smiled knowingly, and it wasn't at Del Boy falling through the open bar counter flap.

It was 8.28 a.m. on Monday, 26 February. Angel opened his office door, went in, closed it, took off his coat, hung it on the peg on the side of the green metal stationery cupboard and then reached out to the phone. He tapped in a number, then pulled faces while fingering through the pile of unopened post on his desk.

Eventually Ahmed answered the phone. 'Good morning, sir.'

'Where have you been, Ahmed?' he grumbled.

'It's not half past yet, sir.'

'Oh, isn't it? Is DS Gawber there?'

'Yes, sir.'

'Tell him I want to see him straight away.'

'Right, sir.'

He replaced the phone and wrote a name and address on a memo pad and tore the page off.

A minute or so later, there was a knock at the door and Gawber came in.

'Come in, Ron. You needn't sit down.' He gave him the memo. 'I want you to get a warrant, then arrest this man at this address and bring him in. You'd better take somebody with you. I should take Scrivens.'

Gawber looked at the memo. His mouth dropped open. 'Shall I charge him with *both* murders, sir?'

'Yes. Go armed. And be quick about it before he commits a third.'

It was 9.00 a.m. the following morning, Tuesday, 27 February. Gawber had completed his mission the previous day and was talking over the case in Angel's office.

'It's like that politician said, sir.'

Angel frowned. 'What politician? There's so many of 'em and they say so much.'

Gawber screwed up his face as he tried to remember. 'Something like, "One man's pay rise is another man's pay freeze."'

Angel looked up. 'It was Harold Wilson,' he replied with a sniff.

'That's right, sir.'

'He also said that the pound in your pocket will remain the same. Tell that to the old age pensioners. But you're correct, Ron. It's an indisputable fact that if someone loses, then somebody else must win. That's what double column entry bookkeeping is all about. To say that nobody is a winner in a commercial transaction is the talk of a fool or a con man. That's what gave him away. When he said, "Nobody wins," I knew he was lying, but at the time, I couldn't see *why* he was lying.'

'Like the man with the white rabbit, you were telling me about, sir. The man with clean hands, who didn't stroke the rabbit, was the liar.'

'Exactly. Anyway, I spoke to Euromagna's insurance company and they admitted that they would be obligated to pay out if the film had to be abandoned due to the serious illness, accident or death of a principal actor or director that prevented him/her from working or performing to the required standard during the thirteen weeks contract period (in this case) of the making of the film. If the insurance company had needed any additional reason, I reckon he would have murdered Nanette Quadrette and Otis Stroom and worked his way all the way down to the studio tea lady!'

Gawber nodded sombrely, knowing that it was probably true.

'Grant Montague's personal share after expenses as a director of the company would have been over two and a half million. Violet Buhl at the escort agency, after some threat of blackmail on my part, admitted that she wanted two million to buy herself out of the business. When neither

Mark Johannson nor Alexander Bernedetti would play ball and obligingly leave the Edgar Poole project voluntarily in exchange for a hand out of half a million, Montague had by then shot his mouth off and had to murder them or his world would have fallen in. He might have got away with it, too.'

Gawber nodded his understanding. 'He wasn't banking on you, sir,' Gawber said with a little cough.

Angel sighed. 'Haven't you got rid of that cough yet?' he said impatiently.

'What did "Agapoo" mean, sir?' he said, ignoring the question.

Angel smiled. 'It was simply what Harry Hull thought he heard when Grant Montague said "Edgar Poole". Agapoo. Got it?'

'Ah!' Gawber said with a big smile. Then he coughed again, several times. He took the small bottle out of his pocket. 'Excuse me, sir,' he said as he took a sip.

'You really should go to the doctor's!' Angel said impatiently.

'It's only a cough.'

The phone rang. Angel reached out for it.

It was the woman civilian on the switchboard. She sounded different. Her usual bored, mechanical drone and overt rudeness was missing. 'There's a woman, sounds young, on the line,' she said spiritedly and an octave higher than her usual level. 'Seems to be in some trouble or other. She's asking for you. I couldn't get her name. Says it's *desperately* urgent!'

Angel's heart began to pound. 'Put her through.'

Gawber raised his head. He could sense something was wrong.

There was a click.

'Is that Inspector Angel?' a girl's quivering voice said.

'Yes. Who's that?'

'I am in desperate trouble. I've been imprisoned by a man. I don't know who he is. He knows you, I know *that*. He intends holding me ransom, he says, for some thing very valuable. Treasure, he says. Treasure that should have come to him. Oh dear. Please, Inspector, get me out of here.'

'Where are you?'

'I don't know. I'm in a cold, dark cellar. It's pitch black. It's horrible. Oh please, get me out of here. I don't know where it is. He's dangerous and as mad as a hatter. Oh. I'll have to go. I can hear him coming back.'

'Don't cancel the call. Leave the line open. Who are you? What's your name?'

She didn't reply. Through the phone he could hear a big heavy bang of a steel door. In the distance a man's voice shouted something; it was loud, seemed to be aggressive but indistinguishable. Then, as he came nearer to the mobile, Angel made out the words, 'Give me that phone'.

The woman yelled, 'No.'

There was a scream.

Angel's lips tightened back against his teeth. The back of his hand turned to gooseflesh.

The line went dead.

Angel didn't replace the handset.

'What is it?' Gawber said.

Angel wondered whether he should attempt to ring back. He decided that it might make the caller's position difficult and maybe even endanger her life. He slapped down the phone. Angel jumped up, 'A woman abducted, Ron. I think I know where she might be. Come on,' he said pulling open the office door. 'Get two torches from CID. I'll tell you all about it in the car.'

The two men ran out of the office.

SIXTEEN

'The man's voice, I am certain, was that of David Schuster,' Angel said when they were in the BMW and racing down to the old mill. 'And the girl's description of where she was being held perfectly matched the small cellar at the far end of the basement under his shop.'

Gawber's eyebrows shot up. 'I remember it. Shouldn't we have withdrawn handguns from the armoury, sir? We don't know what we might meet in the darkness of the place?'

'He's not known to carry arms. We don't know what danger the girl might be in. It would have taken us valuable time filling in the applications.'

Gawber nodded. On reflection, he had to agree. 'Who is the girl?'

'No idea.'

Angel stopped the car outside the main door of the old stone mill building, which had experienced so much activity these past few days. He slammed the car door. Gawber brought the torches and handed one to him. They rushed up the three steps through the damaged door and inside the old mill. It was cold. Angel could have sworn it was colder inside than it was outside in the street. They switched on the powerful torches and began the descent to the cellar. Every step he took, Angel wondered what he might find. He was beginning to think that David Schuster had finally blown his top and was ready for the funny farm. He had seen it happen many times in his job. It was very sad. And it always seemed to happen to small people. Well, Schuster wasn't actually small, he was medium sized, but small in comparison to the average in any gathering of policemen.

They reached the basement floor and flashed the lights along the big expanse. They looked ahead at the steel door in the wall at the far end. It was closed as before. The two men looked at each other. Everything was as quiet as ashes in an urn on the mantelpiece.

Angel licked his lips. He was beginning to have doubts. He wondered if he had properly deduced that this was the place where the phone call had come from.

Neither of the policemen saw a figure manoeuvre stealthily round a pillar to keep in the shadows as they made a beeline for the steel door at the far end.

They reached it and listened outside the little cell. Absolute silence. Angel grabbed the door handle and pulled it open. He waved to Gawber to go in. Gawber looked through the gap. He went inside and flashed the torch around. Angel pulled the heavy door open even further. There was nobody in the cell, but there was something else, something unexpected, lying flat on the stone-built table in the middle of the little room. Angel saw it also. It was a small suitcase. It was closed. It was old and well-used.

Angel came in and let the door close. It closed with a loud, disconcerting clang and echo. He crossed to the suitcase. As he did so, there was the squeak of a key turning in a rusty lock and then a metallic thud as the bolt sprang out. The sound was unmistakable.

The two men stared at each other for a second, realized what they had heard, then rushed at the steel door. They pushed hard at it. It didn't move. They tried again, harder. It didn't even shake. They knew they were well and truly imprisoned.

'It's Schuster,' Angel said.

Gawber coughed. He dipped into his pocket, took out the bottle and took a sip from it.

Angel yelled, 'Schuster! What are you doing? Why have you locked us in here? What do you want? What's going on? It doesn't make sense. Where's the girl? If you've harmed her, you'll pay for it.'

They waited. There was no reply.

'Are you there, Schuster?' Angel yelled again.

He was certain the man was out there, close to the other side of the door … listening. He could almost hear him breathing. Seconds later they heard footsteps as the man strode quickly away.

Angel rubbed his chin. He turned to Gawber. 'Where is the girl? Who the hell is she? Has he murdered her?'

Gawber coughed, then he said, 'Don't know, sir.'

'Get on your mobile and get somebody to let us out of here. And tell them to be on the lookout for David Schuster. Warn them that he's still in the area.'

Gawber didn't hesitate. With shaking hands, he dialled the station and spoke to Ahmed, who said he would notify uniform immediately.

Meanwhile, Angel flashed his torch around the little cell and then moved in on the suitcase. He slid the two catches sideways with his thumbs and the fasteners clicked up. He raised the suitcase lid and shone his torch inside.

Then he had the shock of his life.

He saw the dial of a big, old-fashioned alarm clock, fastened to four wires sticking out through Blu-Tack, the tops of two double AA batteries and six sticks that looked like candles covered in cream paper, wrapped together with adhesive tape, which on closer examination proved to be dynamite.

Angel's pulse raced up to 200, his mouth went as dry as a box of feathers. He backed away from the suitcase. 'Ron! It's a bomb,' he said quietly.

'A bomb?' Gawber yelled.

Angel looked anxiously round the small cell as his heart banged like a drum through his shirt. 'We've got to get out of here.'

Gawber glanced across at the suitcase on the stone table. The lid was open. He took in the features of the primitive time bomb. Angel saw him and came back to look at it.

They could hear it ticking. Only just. It was a quiet, devious tick.

The alarm hand was set at six o'clock and the other hands were set at three minutes to six.

'I suppose when the alarm bell rings, the circuit will be closed and the bomb will …' Angel didn't finish the sentence.

'We've three minutes,' Gawber stammered, '… to get out of here.'

Angel shook his head. 'We *can't* get out of here. Look at that door. The walls are two or three feet thick. And there are no windows. Hmm. We've got to disarm this thing.'

Gawber's face went white. 'How?'

'I don't know *how*,' he snapped. 'If we had some wire cutters or scissors.'

'No. Nothing like that, sir.'

'If we had a screwdriver, we could stick it in the clock works and hope to stop the works.'

'We've no cutting tools. No screwdriver.'

Angel ran his hand through his hair, then quickly turned back. 'Ron. Empty your pockets. Let's see what we *do* have.'

Both of the men quickly put all their belongings on the stone table next to the suitcase. Wallet, ID, money, keys, handkerchief, ballpoint pen, notebook, wristwatches … Gawber, lastly, put the bottle of cough medicine on the pile.

He was looking for something to halt the clock mechanism. A pen wasn't strong enough to pierce the dial front.

Angel glanced at the clock dial. It showed one minute and forty-five seconds to go. He didn't remark on it. It was obvious, and he thought Ron Gawber had taken about as much pressure as he could bear. He was coughing more frequently. It was very worrying.

Then his eyes suddenly lit up. He shone his torch down to the floor. By the walls was a sprinkling of sand, grains that had fallen away over the years from the crumbling of the sandstone walls.

'Quick, Ron. Collect up this sand dust. As much as you can.'

Gawber didn't question why. He gathered up the small amount that there was, into the palm of his hand.

'That's enough. Is that clock still ticking?'

'Yes.'

Gawber transferred his collection of sand into Angel's hand. Angel reached out for the bottle of cough medicine. It was about a third full. He put all the sand and dust they had collected inside the bottle and shook it up. Then with trembling hands, he poured the gritty, sticky substance over the clock dial. He emptied the bottle and banged the base of it with his other hand to get out every last drop.

'Clocks don't like grit, Ron. Let's hope they don't like this?'

The clock continued to tick. The second hand had only one more 360 degree sweep of the dial to make before it would hit six o'clock.

They anxiously watched the runny mess make its way round the edges of the dial and then disappear underneath into the mechanics of the clock. It was a very long shot and Angel knew it.

'There's nothing more I can think of, Ron,' he said, holding his hands out over the suitcase and shaking his head.

'No,' Gawber said, still staring at the clock dial and listening to the ominous tick of the clock.

'Thirty seconds,' Angel said. He put a hand on his chest and prayed.

'We should get under the table, sir. It's the best shelter there is,' Gawber said crouching down and scrambling underneath.

Angel grunted, but he couldn't take his eyes off the clock face. All the syrupy mud had now run off the dial into the workings of it. It simply needed one minuscule spec of grit to find its way between a cog and a sprocket, or between any two meshing gear wheels, and the clock would stop, the bomb wouldn't detonate and he would have to wait for another time to find out whether his final destination was heaven or hell.

'Come on.' Gawber said from underneath the stone table. 'There's plenty of room.'

Angel thought that with a charge of six sticks of dynamite, it wouldn't make much difference in that small cellar whether he was under the table or stood where he was.

There were now only ten seconds left. He watched the slim, black, second hand, edge jerkily round the dial. Fifty-five, fifty-six, fifty-seven, and then it stopped.

Angel stared at it, hardly daring to believe his eyes. He held his breath. He listened for the ticking; that too, had stopped.

It had worked.

He gave a very heavy sigh. And then another. Then he bent down and looked under the table. He saw Gawber rolled into a ball, gripping his torch in one hand, the other hand over an ear and his eyes shut.

He nudged him. 'Come on, Ron. I think we're OK.'

Gawber opened his eyes and blinked. 'Did it work?'

Angel grinned. 'I always said I'd find a better use for that cough medicine of yours.'

Gawber unrolled himself, stood up and stretched his arms. Then he looked cautiously inside the open suitcase. 'Wow! Only three seconds to go?'

Suddenly they heard several sets of footsteps outside and voices.

Angel squeezed Gawber's arm and said, 'Shh!' He didn't know if Schuster or some other villain had returned for some reason.

They listened at the steel door. They heard a familiar voice. 'DI Angel are you there? It's Ahmed, sir. Are you there?'

Angel and Gawber looked at each other and smiled.

'The cavalry has arrived.'

Angel battered on the steel door. 'In here, Ahmed. Behind this steel door. Can you unlock it? Is the key in the lock?'

'No, sir.'

Gawber sighed.

Ahmed and a squad of uniformed worked quickly to release the two men. They had to get crow bars and a welder to release them. The whole operation took more than an hour.

Angel told Ahmed to phone the UXB unit in York and tell them that there really *was* a bomb this time, a homemade unexploded bomb!

Ahmed nodded. He was also told to organize a guard of the place until the army arrived. Then Angel and Gawber rushed out of the cellar and up the steps to discover that all four tyres of Angel's car had been slashed. Angel got a patrol car to take them to the police station.

'That was a near miss, sir. I'm glad to be away from that place.'

'Schuster is nothing if he's not thorough,' Angel said as the driver pulled onto the main road.

Gawber looked very tired.

'I suppose Schuster would be thinking that his plan had worked,' Angel said. 'That his bomb had gone off, and that we are dead.'

Gawber nodded.

'So what would he be up to now?'

'He would know he couldn't stay any longer at the shop, sir. He'd be wanted by the police. He'd really want to get away from the place.'

'*Right* away from the place. Well away from Bromersley too.'

'Yes, sir.'

'But he doesn't have a car, and he doesn't drive. That's why he didn't take mine.'

'So he'd need transport. If he proposes a long journey, he'd need a taxi either to a train station, say Doncaster or Leeds, or to an airport, Leeds/Bradford or Robin Hood.'

'Exactly. Shouldn't be difficult. Crack on with it. Must catch him before he gets out of the country. Must find the taxi he took.'

'Right, sir,' Gawber said.

The patrol car drove up to the front of the station.

'Wait here for us, lad,' Angel called to the patrol-car driver as he opened the door.

The two men ran up the steps to reception and were waved through the security door. They dashed into Angel's office. Angel pulled the local directory out of a drawer. There were six taxi firms in the town and four others in villages a few miles out. Angel decided initially to discount the ones out of town. Gawber noted the top three numbers and dashed off to the CID office to use the phone. Angel took the bottom three and began tapping in a number.

In four minutes, Gawber came running into Angel's office all smiles. He had found Schuster. A driver at the third taxi firm he had phoned had picked up a man answering Schuster's description with a young woman outside the old mill building about an hour ago and had taken them to Leeds/Bradford airport. In fact, the dispatcher had spoken to the driver by radio while Gawber was on the line. He had told him he thought they were a honeymoon couple. They had two suitcases with them.

Angel beamed and jumped up. 'Great,' he said, then frowned. 'Bring your handcuffs,' he said meaningfully and he reached into a drawer, took out his own pair and pushed them into his pocket.

'Right, sir.' Gawber went back to his desk to collect his and the two men dashed out of the offices and up the corridor. They jumped into the car, instructed the driver to take them to the airport as quickly as possible, then sat back in the seat to catch their breath.

'Honeymoon couple, eh?' Angel said thoughtfully.

'That's what he said, sir.'

A few miles later, Angel said, 'You know, Ron. We've been had. The phone call from the desperate young woman was a good bit of acting, to get us into that cellar.'

'Aye, to get shot of us,' Gawber said.

'Damn well nearly succeeded too.'

'Who is the girl?'

'The only girl I can think of is the one who dropped the candle-snuffer while coming over Mace's garden wall.'

'Yes, sir. Slim, black hair, boys' socks.'

'That's her. Who the hell is she?'

Thirty-five minutes later, their driver pulled into the car park at Leeds/Bradford airport. Angel and Gawber showed their ID and found themselves in the departure lounge. They scanned it quickly, but there was no sign of Schuster with or without a young woman. They went up to the departure gate, showed their ID to airport police and after some argument and questioning they were allowed through. They rushed out onto the tarmac. There were two planes loading passengers. Short queues of people were dribbling slowly across the tarmac onto the steps to the planes. He wondered if they were too late.

Suddenly, Angel spotted a dapper little man with a beautiful dark-haired girl on his arm crossing the short distance to the bottom step of a plane.

His heart leapt. His pulse raced. 'They are there, Ron,' Angel said, 'I'll take Schuster. You take the girl, Flavia Radowitz!'

'Just thought you'd like to know that the BDU arrived about an hour ago and are dealing with the UXB at the mill, sir,' Ahmed said as he placed the cup of tea on the desk in front of him.

Angel frowned. 'What's the BDU? Have you started making these shorthand initial letters up yourself now?'

'No sir,' he said, looking surprised. 'Bomb Disposal Unit.'

Angel grinned. 'All right, Ahmed. Thank you.'

Gawber knocked and came in. Ahmed went out and closed the door.

'At a rough estimate, sir,' Gawber began, 'there's £80,000 worth of old gold, antique jewellery, Georgian silver and ivory bits and pieces in David Schuster's suitcases. He says it's all been acquired honestly through twenty-two years trading in his shop.'

Angel nodded and said, 'I'm inclined to believe that much.'

'He could have set himself up very well indeed with Flavia Radowitz in Rio de Janiero.'

Angel took a sip of the tea. 'If she didn't take it off him first,' he grinned over the top of the cup.

Gawber smiled. 'You knew it was her, didn't you, sir?'

'I *thought* it was. I couldn't understand why a girl would want to wear boys' socks, then it came to me. It was a way to cover that big tattoo on her ankle. A tattoo of a tarantula that size, in that place, would have identified her in a flash.'

Gawber nodded. 'Of course.'

The phone rang. He reached out for it. 'Angel.'

It was Harker. 'You'd better come up here. I've got some news for you.'

Angel wrinkled his nose. Now what? 'Right, sir.' Angel dashed up the corridor, knocked on his door and went in.

'Aye, come in. Sit down, Michael.'

Angel blinked. The honey monster was being nice. He called him by his first name. There must be a catch somewhere. He knew to be wary.

'Yes, sir?'

'Ah yes,' Harker said, rubbing his bony hands together like an undertaker at a meeting of the nonagenarian society. 'I've had a phone call from Lord Truscott.'

Angel pursed his lips. He couldn't quite recall the name. He was certain he hadn't met him. He raised his eyebrows. 'Oh yes, sir,' he said, to keep the story going.

'Most thankful he was. He's sending you a cheque, he says. A reward, he said, for finding two most valuable paintings of his.'

Angel remembered. Matthew Elliott had mentioned him. The naked ladies with the fat backsides. His face brightened. 'Very good of him, sir.'

'Yes,' the monster said. 'For £3000.'

Angel's face glowed. '£3000!'

'Of course, I thanked him profusely on your behalf, and had to explain to him, as I know you would have done, that members of the force cannot accept personal reward for doing what, after all, is their duty, and that you would, of course, donate it to the Bromersley Police Charity.'

Angel wrinkled his nose. He was desperately thinking of some reason why an exception might be made to negate the rule in this case, but he couldn't actually think of anything.

'So, Michael, when you get the cheque, pay it into your account and then make a cheque out to Bromersley Police Charity for £2,800 and everybody will be satisfied, won't they?'

THE END

OTHER BOOKS BY ROGER SILVERWOOD

YORKSHIRE MURDER MYSTERIES

Book 1: THE MISSING NURSE
Book 2: THE MISSING WIFE
Book 3: THE MAN IN THE PINK SUIT
Book 4: THE MORALS OF A MURDERER
Book 5: THE AUCTION MURDERS
Book 6: THE MISSING KILLER
Book 7: THE UMBRELLA MURDERS
Book 8: THE MISSING MILLIONAIRE
Book 9: THE MISSING THIEF

FREE KINDLE BOOKS

Please join our mailing list for free Kindle crime thriller, detective, mystery, romance books and new releases! www.joffebooks.com

JOFFE BOOKS

Thank you for reading this book. If you enjoyed it please leave feedback on Amazon, and if there is anything we missed or you have a question about then please get in touch. The author and publishing team appreciate your feedback and time reading this book.

Our email is office@joffebooks.com

Follow us on facebook www.facebook.com/joffebooks

We're very grateful to eagle-eyed readers who take the time to contact us. Please send any errors you find to corrections@joffebooks.com

Printed in Dunstable, United Kingdom

64224341R00099